ADVENTURES WITH THE SHORTIEZ

Portal to the Unknown World

Creola Thomas

CONTENTS

THE MOST DISASTROUS, OUTRAGEOUS, DOWNRIGHT RIDICULOUS DAY OF MY LIFE

My name is Salle with an E, not a Y. See, the reason this is important is that I was named after my Big Mama, and she was a boss in a small town. My mother called her a big fish in a small pond, but she held down the business, whatever her business was. Most people say we are a lot alike because I can be bossy. I wouldn't say that I'm bossy, but *somebody's* gotta take charge, and it might as well be me.

Seems like every time I lay low, something *horrible* happens. The horrible set of mishaps I'm about to describe landed me and my crew in a strange place, which even now is hard to explain. Before I tell you about that place, let me just tell you that there are hidden portals in the hood, worlds with talking creatures with motives and purposes yet to unfold. A world undefined by anything you have ever seen or heard before. This place doesn't only live in the imaginations of the youth or the elderly or the insane—it's more than just imagination.

I am warning you early to brace yourself, hold on tight for dear life, as if you were at the top of a hundred-foot drop on an amusement park ride, excitedly waiting and dreadfully anticipating the story I will tell you soon. This whole tale of twisted events will leave you twiddling your thumbs, lost in thought, half wanting to believe they're true. But they were experienced by four other people, and therefore, there must be some truth to them, right? A real-life mystery.

My mother says that there's no such thing as mysteries, that everything has a logical explanation. She says that if you ever think you've found a mystery, you're just not the right person to solve it. The answer is out there, just waiting on the right person.

I may have to disagree with my mother on this. Of course, I am only thirteen, but as sure as I am the only girl in my family, I experienced a mystery, and if I have to wait for the rest of my life, I hope to meet the right person who will unravel this one.

It all started two weeks before seventh grade was to end. We were in the science lab getting our final projects together. Well, some of us were working hard on our projects, like Marion, Sharie, and me. Ryan, however, was dancing with the skeleton, and Stinky—who really shouldn't have been there because he is three years younger and a whole lot dumber—was mixing all sorts of liquids together, all sorts of science stuff. Sharie and I hoped he would stop, but he didn't. He really didn't feel like he had to listen to us. We were just a couple of shortiez from the streets, like him, trying to make it to middle school next year.

Ryan couldn't resist all the fun Stinky was having, so he decided to join him. The two of them were making some sort of magic potion that would surely bring about world peace one day. We didn't pay it much mind because we were deep in our own work, but then the smell of burned rubber began to fill the air. After that came a foul odor. We went over to see what kind of concoction those clowns were making, and suddenly, everything went *kaboom!* They had mixed popping powder with baking soda and vinegar in one of the large silver pots on the science table. The next thing I know, popping gunfire sounds were coming from everywhere!

Then suds-like bubbles began to fill the air, and when they burst, they actually stained the walls, desks, and cabinets. The boys must have added something foamy white to the potion because white smoky clouds merged with giant smelly puffs, and together, those took to the air, covering everything in white wherever they landed. Marion tried to turn off the heating stove, but the smelly bubbles popping all over the place were also gummy and sticky, and as he was on his way to simply calm down the situation, he slipped, fell on top of the skeleton, and bones flew all over the place.

In his struggle to get back up, he knocked down the bookcase and the big blue globe went spinning into the classroom window. The mysterious exploding sandwich bags tumbled off the top bookcase. Our science teacher, Mr. Scott, had said that if those ever dropped it would sound like an atomic bomb, and boy, he didn't lie. Those little exploding plastic bags not only let out a loud banging sound but also had a unique smell, like roach spray or Mr. Lewis's stinky cologne.

Well, what's a girl to do? This was a man-made disaster, and the two boys who created it were huddled under a table covered in something that could have at some point been baking soda. I slipped trying to get to the intercom and slid all the way across the room, knocking down books, a desk, measuring glasses full of thermometers, plastic bottles, Petri dishes, and magnifiers, before finally reaching the garbage can. Heck, even my head took the initiative to mop up some of the suds and was completely white on top. You would think I had prematurely gone gray.

In the midst of all this, my mind was in panic mode as it lingered on my mom's reaction—I imagined the hundred and one different ways she was going to kill me for messing up the French braids she had just paid a neighbor to do for me. Sharie managed to ring for help, but not before she slid into the window shades, pulling them down and covering herself in curtains, spiders, and a whole lot of hidden dust. The smelly floating fart bubbles greeted all of us several times with a gentle kiss, leaving our faces, backs, and necks covered in tar glue and smelling like rotten eggs.

On top of all that, when help arrived, Ryan and Stinky—the originators of this whole mess—weren't the only ones in trouble. We *all* got marched down the hall to meet our doom. In one single-file line, heads bowed, the kids most of the community affectionately referred to as simply "dem shortiez" were definitely taking the walk of shame. Disgruntled and disheveled, we walked the long hall. Every now and again, Sharie, Marion, and I gave Ryan and Stinky the evil eye — making sure they were well aware this was all their fault and that we were expecting them to clear the rest of us of any wrong.

Now, this is not the first time we've taken the long walk to Principal Morten's office, but we had hoped that maybe, just maybe, by this time we had seen our last detention … until eighth grade, of course. This was quickly becoming *the most disastrous, outrageous, downright ridiculous day of my life.*

2

THE VERDICT IS IN—LET'S HANG 'EM! I MEAN, BOOK 'EM!

Principal Morten of St. Joseph's Catholic School was a jolly middle-aged dude who had eaten a few more doughnuts than salads. He had obviously done more socializing than exercising, but he listened twice as much as he spoke, and for that, we pitied and adored him. Principal Morten was known for his uncompromising compassion. Even in his anger, he exhibited kindness. He was like a judge who never found anyone totally guilty.

One of the security guards, acting as if he was the Secret Service or something, showed him a few visuals of the room we had just destroyed. Even if he hadn't seen the room, we were living proof of the destruction.

Stinky, covered in his own funk, was especially blasted by his own self-made fart bombs. He looked as if he'd been hit several times, and when they landed on him, they changed color, making him look like the rainbow stink boy. He also had black mud stripes all over his face and hands. Ryan, the once-white kid with fiery red hair, was now covered in a mix of dark-colored mud and white chalky powder. His hair was no longer red, but rather a musty yellow. Marion had rips in his shirt from one of the skeleton bones, and he had mud stains all over his face and clothes.

Sharie, who had to brush a few baby spiders out of her hair, sat traumatized and silent. She twitched every free second or so. I knew she was throwing up hiccups when she started jerking her head back. *Poor Sharie*, I thought. I decided not to tell her a dead spider was trapped between her hair and barrette because I knew, from the moment she arrived in the office, that she was on the verge of having a panic attack.

Lastly, there was me, Miss Gray Hair—smelly, muddy, and missing a sock and shoe from trying to recuse myself from the disastrous event that had just invaded my life. I heard the sirens from the fire trucks which slowly accompanied the truth of another reality—that the smoking blue-and-red stuff that sparked like electricity was actually fire, and we had, of course, burned down part of the newly decorated science lab. Yeah, that's going to *really* help our stellar reputation with the community.

Principal Morten mulled over the pictures, every now and again giving us a sneak peek of his disappointment by looking up, eyeing us closely, and shaking his head. From time to time, he would grunt words no one understood. He was restraining himself. I've got to tell you, this was not regular old Principal Morten. He is usually more preachy in these matters, but he was quiet—a little too quiet—and I got the feeling that it wasn't because he was praying. Ryan, being braver than he had to be, finally spoke the words we were all longing to hear him say:

"Father …"

He was going in for the appeal … and he was going to cry. Yes! Score! If you cried, Principal Morten would give you a break. Also, when you addressed him as "Father," instead of "Principal," it meant you wanted compassion, and with all the damage done to that room, we needed more than compassion—we needed a Jesus-walking-on-water miracle. Even though it appeared that Principal Morten was not quite ready to hear from any of us, Ryan took his silence as permission to speak.

With trembling lips and a teardrop hiding in the corner of his large green eyes, waiting to fall on cue, Ryan continued. "Father ... Father, I know things look really bad in there, but it really wasn't supposed to turn out that way."

Oh, no, I thought, *what is he doing?* I wanted to hear begging and pleading. I wanted to see tears, lots of tears. We all knew the lingo. The routine was not new to us, especially not new to Ryan. We were all sort of known for making mishaps every now and again. I paid closer attention as he began speaking again, and this time, I hoped to see some showmanship.

"First of all, it wasn't everyone who created this mess. You see, Stinky and me, sir, we were trying to be inventors, like Carver, so we had to be daring. But we are *so* sorry! Please, please don't kick us out."

The tears began to flow like a faucet and I could hear an angelic choir singing. If I didn't know Ryan, I would have believed him. We were sure to get a pass this time, maybe even a hero's reward. I mean, not to brag or anything, but a few of us did try to salvage the situation.

Principal Morten turned his attention totally away from us, walked to the cabinet, and got out a large black container labeled "Drake Shortiez." Yeah, that was us alright. The container was big and packed with pink slips. What was he doing, saving our detention slips as souvenirs? Principal Morten picked out one of the slips and turned to face Ryan.

"What happened with the car, Ryan?"

"The car, sir?" Ryan repeated as if he didn't understand the word *car*. "Well, I will tell you what happened with the car. It was a rainy Chicago day, and we shortiez were walking home from school, like most days, but on this day, we didn't have umbrellas, so our sweater and jackets were our covering, and everything from the top to the bottom was wet ..."

As Ryan spoke, my mind drifted back to that soggy fall day. I could feel the rain soaking through my clothes all over again, and I could hear Stinky saying, "Let's wait in that car until the rain slows down—my bones hurt."

We had come across a block car in the rain: one of those busted-down cars in the hood that just sit there waiting to get towed. Sometimes they attract suspicious activity, but today was a whole other story.

"Yeah, I bet your bones hurt!" I teased Stinky. After a little convincing, we all packed in the car, glad to get out of the rain.

Out of nowhere, Ryan starts boasting, "I can drive this car."

"No you can't," Stinky challenged.

"Yes, I can too. I can make it start."

Marion tried to intervene, but before anyone could say anything, Ryan popped that hood and started moving some things about. He took out the ignition key, arranged the cords, and low and behold, like a common car thief he made the ignition activate. With us all in shock, he announces confidently, "I can drive this piece of crap too—move over." Well, after seeing him in action under the hood, who would doubt that he could? Marion moved out of the driver's seat and jumped in the back. And with no sense at all, Ryan zoomed out into the street.

I could have died that day. I saw my life float by like the glass bottles floating around us down the street. Ryan drove that car alright— right into the back of a funeral home, which let in the rising floodwater and let out several empty caskets, which drifted down the streets like decorated floats in a parade. The darn car stopped, and then caught fire. What more could a group of kids do but try and float on the caskets, as the water was all of twelve feet, and we could have drowned?

Okay, it was more like two feet, but we had to get home somehow, or people would have known we burned up the block car, and for the record, block cars are supposed to be undrivable. Ryan knew that admitting to the car situation could land him in a lot of hot water, but it just so happened all the caskets were recovered, and no harm was done. The block car still sits there. The rain put out the fire, and someone simply pushed it back into place.

Ryan's stammering brought my mind back to Principal Morten's office. Ryan couldn't think of anything quick to say, so he said what we all probably would have said: "Sir, I don't know much about cars. That wasn't me!"

At this point, Principal Morten took out a picture someone had given him of Ryan — eyes the size of bow dollars, mouth opened wide driving — yes — a car. We all got to view what appeared to be exhibit one. We got up quietly from our seats and looked at the picture, which was undeniably Ryan — and of course, us — and with the precision of choreographed dancers, we all took two steps back to our chairs and hoped that the conversation about the car would end. Principal Morten shook his head but said no more about the car.

I saw it: it didn't linger long, but I'd say anger — not disappointment, but anger —

flashed through Principal Morten's eyes as he removed another pink slip from the box.

"Tell me about the corner store situation."

Marion stood up and announced, "We are not guilty! Kids go in that store and steal all the time and get chased out. Everybody thinks we are so bad, but what about *love*?"

Principal Morten eyed him carefully, as this was a new thing Marion was doing (it was a new *something* alright). I didn't know where he was going with this.

"Yes, Father Morten, these little shortiez just need *love*, that's all," Principal Morten slapped down a photo of Stinky putting bags of chips in his backpack, front pants pockets, and back pockets. Again, we all got up and looked at the pictures and quickly sat back down. All I was thinking was, *please don't let Stinky open his mouth*. Maybe we're a little on the bad side, but if we just keep quiet, Principal Morten would simply give us a paper to write over the summer and we'd be all good. But nooooo! Stinky had to open his BIG, FAT mouth.

"Well, actually, sir, I wasn't stealing anything. I didn't know he didn't have a layaway plan."

"Layaway plan?" asked Principal Morten.

"Yeah, I wasn't stealing the stuff, I was just putting it on layaway. I had every intention of paying him later. If he wouldn't have grabbed me by the collar, taken the chips and all from me, and forced me to run for my very life, I would have told him, 'Look dude, I'll pay you later.'"

"Pay him later?" Principal Morten repeated because he, like the rest of us, couldn't believe what Stinky was claiming. But the more we thought about it, the more we were like, *I wonder if that store did have a layaway plan?*

"I am disappointed and saddened by this series of events. Really, really sad." He stopped — and our hearts stopped, too. He spoke again, and we were resuscitated. "In this box, these are your combined detentions."

"Clearly, we are just not doing enough," said Ryan, hoping to bring clarification to his statements, but Principal Morten wasn't having it.

"It's not that you are not doing enough, so stop it, Ryan," he said sternly. "It's my turn to speak. We are not doing enough and you are not doing enough. It's a two-way street. You've got to want to do good."

"We do, Father," I said, hoping that my voice sounded remorseful enough.

"No, clearly you do not!" declared Principal Morten.

Marion, who can be the most rational one of us all, stood up to again defend us (I hoped). One thing for sure is that he knows how to get a situation calmed down with words no one really understands. It has been said that Marion can convince anyone of anything if he believes it himself.

Marion spoke softly, pleading with Principal Morten, "Give us one more chance to prove that we do know how to do good; if we fail, we will spend the whole summer in detention."

"OK," I said, "push pause and reverse, please. Allow me to rewind that last statement. Marion, who is a blockhead, spoke nonsense!" However, Father was seriously taking his plea into consideration.

Finally, Father spoke, "OK, but I am going to give you several chances, because of course, you have done several misdeeds. You are assigned the 'Do Good Challenge.' Within the next two days, you must do at least ten good things collectively, as a group, and have an adult sign off on the deeds. I will be calling each of them to verify the work you did. If you complete the task, no summer detention and you get to stay in this school." In my mind, all I was hearing him say was leave the school—he was kicking us out to public school!

All of a sudden, the image of public school came flying at me as if to slap me back to reality. I saw students throwing books out the window, teachers taking smoke breaks right in the middle of teaching, and kids playing "Punch me out" during the reading block. The image of one of those oversized kids knocking out boys didn't want to leave me—until it was replaced with the image of an oversized girl knocking *me* out. Now, I am a big fish in this small pond, and trust me, I can stand my ground with anyone in a fight, but I just didn't think I could beat up the six-foot-tall Amazon girl who was playing knock-me-out on my face. And poor Sharie, she wouldn't even have a chance. No public school for us, we were just not yet ready for that.

As I tried not to think of Amazon girl, Principal Morten continued: "If you do not complete this task, each of you will spend every single day of your summer cleaning up this place—for free—after which you will spend the remainder of your time in a detention room looking at dull white walls. After that, I will be asking your parents to transfer you all back to public school. If your behavior is only getting worse, maybe a private school is not the right setting for you guys. I will be pulling your scholarships as well, but that goes without saying. So, do we have a deal? And before you answer that, remember I am not offering anything else ... Deal?"

"Man, that sucks! We can't do that!" shouted Stinky.

We all looked at him to say shut up, and with eyes that would kill, but unfortunately, that didn't stop him.

"I'm not going to shut up, you know we can't do good!" Stinky added, as if his first comments weren't bad enough.

Principal Morten lowered his glass and stood bravely, with the feeling of victory swallowing up his soul—you could just see it—as he announced, "Hence the challenge. You guys are going to work together, this time for the good of man. And maybe you will learn that getting everything you want and doing what you want to do is not always a good thing. Just because you can do it does not mean you should. I know it took me a while to get that message, kids, but if we all lived in a place where everyone just did what they wanted to do all the time, most people would fight to get out of that place."

"I wouldn't!" I announced. I *wouldn't* fight to get out of it. No adults telling us what to do, it would be perfect! I looked down, as I knew this was a setup plan for failure. So I said a little more forcefully, "It can't be done with this crew." Then I thought about it. Maybe I should just agree. So I added, "*We* can do good, I mean, I am sure Sharie and I can do good, but the rest of them — they my homies, don't get me wrong, but ain't no good in them, except maybe Marion." Somebody had to say it. *Why y'all looking at me?* I wanted to say, but instead I stood my ground and gave back the dirty looks tossed my way.

"Please, Principal Morten, can we split up? That way we can accomplish more. Let's say me and Sharie and then the boys — yeah, the boys against the girls!" Sharie gave me a sinister nod of agreement, as though she knew the challenge would be like taking candy from a baby.

But good ol' can't-wait-to-have-a-cheeseburger Morten shot that idea right down. "No, you have to do it together, and that is that!"

Sharie, who is deaf, signed to me that she didn't want to take the deal, but I explained to her and the rest of them that this may be the only way out of our predicament. So we laid our hands one on top of the other and made a pact with each other. Then we turned to our beloved principal and sealed the contract with him.

Principal Morten was a man of the law, and he took his contracts very seriously. Legend has it that one of his students signed his mother away on a contract with Mr. Morten and that woman works in the school to this very day. Well, obviously the kid lost the bet, but the point is, never sign a contract with Principal Morten. It's long been rumored that you just can't win with him. The very nature of the contract is that you lose.

Come to think of it, this would be just what the good Principal Morten wants: if we lose, we have to clean up his whole school over the summer, and we get kicked out of his school for fall, and all is well in Morten's world. But what choice did a group of shortiez have? We had two days to do ten good things. We could do it; I knew we could. I felt a *Rocky* motivation infuse my soul, and for the first time, I knew that it was truly possible.

However, we weren't off the hook that easy. We still had to clean up the lab the next day, despite the fact that we accepted the challenge, and our parents would have to know what we did and all about the contract. But things could have been a whole lot worse. My mother and father could have been called up to the school.

Now, my father is a Reverend, but he considers Father Morten to be holier than him *and* my grandfather; it has something to do with Father Morten not taking on a wife in all these years, you know, *grown-up* stuff. So for some strange reason, in the presence of Father Morten, my father can barely talk. He just cries like he lost his best friend, and anything the good priest says is right, and they are all wrong. I don't get it myself, so I can't expect you to understand; just know that watching a grown man trying to explain himself while crying at the same time ain't a pretty sight.

Anywho, we still had to get our parents to sign the contract, which I am sure Principal Morten already knew was coming because I am sure this contract wasn't our idea at all but rather the exact road he wanted to take in order to kick us out of school. "That Principal Morten—" I thought as I looked at his irritating, sideways, oddball presence.

However, that was okay, because this rag-tag crew came from strength. So with confidence, I thought, *Can we do it? Yes, we can! Well, I think we can ... or at best, I hope we can ... come to think of it ... maybe not. Sheesh!*

3

THE RAG-TAG CREW: SALLE
MAY THORNTON'S FAMILY

When people think of us shortiez, they think we were joined at the hip, but actually, that is not exactly true. I am from the Thornton clan, the family of the three P's: my grandfather's name is Percy Thornton, my father's name is Percy Thornton (we call him PT), and my brother's name is Percy Thornton (we call him JR).

My mother, Anna Thornton, is a hat-wearing, heel-clacking first lady of the church. What is a first lady? Glad you asked. The first lady is simply the pastor's wife. My mother is all of five foot two, but she's a powerhouse of a woman with the likable factor working in her favor: she makes everyone feel like having cookies and milk and just chilling out. Well, that is, until you make her mad, which is a side you usually don't see. She isn't angry a lot, but when she is, run for cover—or as my father would put it, hide in the closets.

In the community, they call my mother the "Proverb Lady," I guess because she technically works three jobs. She's a mother, of course, but she also works for the local community public school, which is why we attend private school, and she sells Avon, with the hope of driving a pink Cadillac one day. My dad wants her to give up that Avon job. He says she's her best customer, and honestly, I think he hates the thought of maybe one day having to ride in that pink Cadillac.

I want her to keep the Avon job. Some of my nice earrings, bracelets, and flower-smelling perfumes come from that gig, and it somewhat makes me special in my school when I dress up and I have matching earrings, bracelet, and necklace. I am a walking billboard for Avon products, which actually makes me rather special because my perfumes and cheap jewelry did not come from the corner store.

If my mother is the first lady, my father's got to be a pastor, and he is—Pastor Percy Thornton. He preaches almost every Sunday, and when he is not trying to get people to preach to, he likes to believe he can play golf. On any given Saturday morning, my dad, Uncle Bruce, and a few of the community old-timers like to go out on the green. Well, it's not a real golf course; it's the green lawn behind the park district. I hear if you watch out for the dog poop, you may have the opportunity to hit a hole in one.

Another member of the Thornton Clan is my brother, Percy Jr. What can I say about Percy? Well, for starters, call him JR. He is two years older than me and a lot dumber. To put it nicely, he is a rather stupid boy, and he knows it (really, he does). But everyone—and I do mean everyone—thinks he is the future of this family. He manages to never get in trouble and he is always so proper with his uniforms, low haircut, and friendly greetings. My brother speaks to everyone; even if he doesn't know you, he is going to say, "Good morning." What kind of person makes sure he says good morning to everyone he meets, friend or foe? You should be hanged for such atrocities.

You should hear Ms. Nelson brag on how he is so presidential. "What a nice young boy that Percy Jr. is!" It's not just her. The whole Drake Street thinks he is something special. I would be rich if I got paid every time I hear my brother is headed for greatness. Stupidity, I tell you—no, insanity—and you want to know why I feel this way? I know what eyes whose vision is only made clearer with glasses do not see; I know what great things he is headed for, he told me his dream.

Now, you see, I am mostly considered a misfit, a waste of brain energy, one of "dem shortiez" from the hood. But in reality, my brother, the proper-sounding "I have a dream" speaker and communicator, is a plum idiot; my brother's dream is this—but I'm warning you, before you read any further, his dream is going to turn your stomach, make your head spin, knees shake, and if you are standing you may faint so have a seat—Mr. Greatness's dream is ... Are you ready? Are you sure? Well, here it is ... my brother wants to open a booger factory.

You heard me right, he wants to clone boogers. He likes the taste of his boogers. He eats them behind my parents' back. He thinks his boogers taste good and would taste even better if they were on toast. Oh, not to mention the snot—he feels the snot is like ketchup on fries—the more slimy white stuff covering the boogers, the better.

Now, how will he accomplish this dream? Here's his plan: my brother wants to clone the first booger ever. He figured if sheep can be cloned, so can boogers. How will this grand operation work? Actually, the plan may be workable. You will mail in your boogers and he will clone and pickle them in man-made snot and mail them back to you, like a jar of pickles. You can also have dry boogers mixed with raisins. He told me this vision with a loving twinkle in his eyes and a prideful smile on his face, as if he had just unlocked the secrets to saving the planet.

Even I had to admit he had a workable plan for promoting this ridiculous idea. He was aware enough to know that you gotta somehow eliminate the taboos of eating boogers before this plan can work, much like how people eliminate the grossness around eating roaches. He even took time to look up where roaches are eaten, like in China, where there are many farms that actually sell edible roaches. OK, his level of stupidity runs deep as you can see, but he is thinking, and this I have to give him credit for because, sure enough, he is a total idiot. It would have been nice if he just paid a little attention in third-grade science, because if he had, he would know that a roach is an insect and insects can sometimes be consumed because they are rich in protein and low in carbohydrates.

And how will he get the word out concerning his plan to clone boogers? I've got to give him credit for at least trying to think. Now, to get the word out, his plan is to hire a rich rapper or actress and pay him or her millions of dollars to eat boogers and to put eating boogers in a rap or pop song. This is all it will take for people to run out and clone their boogers.

Now, I know this may seem rude to not pay attention when someone is speaking, like when my brother releases this concept into the atmosphere on lazy Saturday mornings when no one is awake and the Saturday morning cartoons are running reruns. So, I may have helped him just a little to come up with ways in which he can expand this brilliant idea and grow the enterprise. I may have given him the idea of boogers on a bun, or boogers in the bag, boogers n' chips, boogers with cheese, and yelled, "This is my favorite boogers sour cream dip!"

So, in other words, good people of the world, you will one day pay JR to eat your boogers. That will be his contribution to the world. I know what you are thinking — I'm the misfit, the original creator of chaos (as I am lovingly known in the community) — but it goes to show that looks can not only be deceiving, but they can be downright criminal. I am waiting for the day when he asks my parents to put up their soon-to-be-paid-off building and invest in his booger enterprise. I will be there to witness it with my own eyes. Nope, I won't be in jail as some have speculated; I will be sitting right in Grandpa's chair.

Some of you may be thinking, why won't I tell him that those little green things are trapping viruses or bacteria before those pathogens enter your system? Why don't I tell him that these boogers are simply waste, something to be blown out and tossed in the trash can, and that cloning boogers would be very similar to cloning poop? Well, I never want to be a dream killer, and maybe if he stopped stealing my stuff and giving it to his wannabe girlfriends, I would have helped a brother out, but he won't stop, and he don't care, and even if he is caught, he always comes out looking like the good guy; so let's just see how well this plan works out for him.

Moving on to another valued member of the Thornton clan: Uncle Bruce. He was very athletic in his younger days—I hear he was really good at basketball. Now he plays back-of-the-yard golf with my dad. He also fixes cars. He owns his own garage on the avenue. He lives on the third floor with his girlfriend, Pat, and Ryan (more about that story later). My grandpa lives in the garden apartment on paper, but most days he's here with us, eating my mother's food and falling asleep in front of the floor model television; he only really stays in his apartment when my TT comes over. My TT is my grandfather's late-life child by a lady with long red hair and longer fingernails. He got someone pregnant when "the boss" died.

Who was the boss? I saved the best, or shall I say, the baddest, for last. The originator of bad, the hood legend, the one and only Big Salle, my grandmother. She actually started the movement that landed us at 914 N. Drake Street some twenty years ago.

When we moved to this block, every house had grass and the sun greeted the people every morning with smiles. Even when it rained, the sun was out relentlessly, giving hope. The moon hung low enough to give the night light, so bright you would think you were on a movie set; the stars twinkled just before they were to dissolve into the light of the day as daybreak sent its love with peaks of sunlight. People wore straw hats and Kane skirts on those rare summer nights. The fog would move at knee level, and us kids could reach and touch it. It had a misty, gritty feel to it, like pushing backward against the heavy wind. The winter was really winter, with snow kissing and melting on your face, not so cold that you couldn't come out and enjoy a sled ride or a friendly snowball fight; the snow melted under hot ice, leaving a safe passage for people to walk, run, and enjoy the beautiful scenery of snow covering all the ugliness of ordinary life.

People didn't even lock their doors until we moved on Drake Street. I hear Big Mama said we integrated the hate. I am still not sure what that means, but when we came, there were others behind us, on other blocks and across the street. It's like our house put out a visual sign that read, "It's OK for black folk to live here now, and all the other people of the world, it's OK for you to move out." And that's exactly what they did; they moved east, taking the sun, policemen, stores, factories, and pockets with dollar bills with them, but not before they made Big Salle a legend.

My grandmother, my namesake, is a hero or a villain depending on who's telling the story, and believe me, stories were told and told and told. So, here's how the story goes: We migrated from the Near North Side of Chicago from a place called Cabrini. The very fact that she was born in the low-cost housing should have given the friendly new neighbors a warning that maybe this family was not to be messed with. Besides, they say my grandma was something special — she came to the world with a bullet in her mouth. They said she didn't even cry as a baby. She couldn't cry. The doctors had to surgically remove the bullet.

She was a big baby, I'm told, and passed the crawling stages. She was born and just started walking. She was always big and she was always bad. No guy in her neighborhood would dare ask her for anything, rather less a date. Well, my grandpa asked her if she wanted a beer, and she fell madly in love with Percy Thornton because he was unafraid to talk to her. They were in love as best as anyone could be in love with Big Salle. They had two baby boys and life was groovy until Grandpa got the draft card and shipped off to war.

Well, Big Salle wasn't going to slack on her part. While her man was away, she held down the folk. Big Salle started saving and stealing, doing whatever it took to take care of her family—wasn't much a woman could do, but what it was she could do, she did. She ran numbers and guns, and if you didn't pay up, you got crushed. Grandpa was gone for three years, and when he came back, not only was Big Salle almost the richest woman in the hood, but she was the maddest woman or man in the hood.

War has its way on the minds of sanity. I'm told you come back with the ghosts of the soldiers you left overseas. This helped us to understand why Grandpa came back different. He was having night shakes and morning quakes. He took long showers and his eyes never met yours in conversation—he always talked head bowed. Most days, I'm told, he just stayed in his room and itched all the time. Big Salle knew she needed to move her family to a more peaceful part of town, so she used Grandpa's GI Bill and all her cash and bought the house on Drake Street. She also didn't want Grandpa going to the nuthouse because whispers were being heard and people were calling him looney, the same people he accused of being spies.

Anywho, before Big Salle would let them try and claim him insane, she moved on Drake with new faces and basic unknowns and safe from army reporting. These were new lands, and although her fame was spoken of often on the North Side, Drake Street had to learn for themselves. She had to break a few jaws and crush a few bones just to live on the street. My grandma stood every bit of six feet with long black hair and broad shoulders, and when she walked down the street, concrete grounds cracked. That's why today we have horizontal lines in sidewalk concrete grounds.

People moved to the other side of the street so as to not walk past my grandmother—you better not look her in the eyes, you might catch on fire. They say my grandmother was so strong, she fought off three white-hooded gang bangers by herself by throwing one of them under a speeding car. She was so strong, she bent a .45 pistol in half. They even said she shot a guy in the eye.

Now, why would she do all this? Glad you asked. See, we were the first African American family to like integrated Drake Street, so a few nice fellows — friendly dudes in Casper the Friendly Ghost Halloween costumes — well, these nice men liked to start friendly barn fires for new African people in the shape of a cross because they knew my mama loved the Lord. I guess my grandma was just having a bad day, she went outside with a bat and the strength of twenty men and cut that celebration short. You can imagine a few people were hurt.

Well, that was my grandmother — the knife-toting gunslinger and "shut yo mouth" bad mother. I bet you are wondering, how did this hood legend die? Well, she shot herself in the foot, bullet went clear though her foot, and she fell asleep on the porch and died with the gun in her hand. She sat on the porch for two days, and no one wanted to wake her up just in case that puddle of blood surrounding her wasn't from her foot. After about two days, the smell was fumigating the area, and someone had to do it. They had to put my grandmother to rest properly.

Our neighbor, Ms. Nelson—yes, the community gossiper—called the cops and my grandma's body was eventually moved to the morgue. This is how Ms. Nelson became somewhat famous herself. She was credited with helping Big Salle receive a proper grave.

After Big Salle's death, my grandpa had to pull it together. He actually went to the doctor and got medication for his strange condition because he didn't have Grandma to scare it out of him. He also put his boys in church. Every Sunday, he would drop them off with one dollar for the offering. He couldn't attend church himself, you know, with his condition and all he couldn't sit for that long, but he wanted his boys in church because he knew that was what his late wife Big Salle would have wanted. He really loved Big Salle.

Okay, he did mess up, my grandpa, and got that baby who is now my TT, which is short for auntie. Oh, by the way, he actually was kind of famous because he was on television denying the baby until the test results came back, and they tell me his pissed his pants right in court. It was a hard laugh for years around here. They say all he could do was look and stare, couldn't even answer any more of the judge's questions.

He just stood there, buck eyes, mouth open, peeing his pants. I would have loved to see this myself, but Grandpa had lawyers have it removed from the world—the tape and the television show just disappeared, gone for life.

OK, St. Joseph, how did I get there? The school is how we all met. I had two really good things going for me and one maybe not-so-much-of-a-good thing. The not-so-good thing was I was much too much like my grandmother (absent of the strength and size), so my parents didn't want me to go to public school. They feared for my life. Somebody was surely going to shut me up one day, and my brother would not be any help.

The two good things are that I was smart—I mean really smart, some would even say a genius—and I could also play the violin. I just picked it up and started playing like a pro. In fact, the Chicago symphony wanted me to be a guest violist, but my mother said no, because she didn't want people throwing tomatoes at me on the stage, even though she knows the only person who would probably throw the tomatoes would be Granddad. Well, he said he would, and we all believed him.

Now, the only school in my area with a good music program, small classroom sizes, and stable teachers was the Catholic school, St.

Joseph's. My mother applied for a scholarship for my brother and me, and it was granted. My dumb brother and I were the first students of color to attend this Catholic grade school from Drake Street, but more would follow. In fact, it was this school that would eventually connect this rag-tag crew, lovely referred to as "dem shortiez."

4

qᛚ☞

THE RAG-TAG CREW: WHO IS RYAN?

It was a summer day, but not just any summer day—the kind of day where heat is too hot to move, so when it lands on you, it penetrates your skin and you feel like you are literally being cooked to order on the spot. I will, on my honor, tell Ryan O'Conner's migration to Drake Street just as he tells it. Why? Because he's my cousin, and I love to hear him tell this story. I think he may even believe it.

Anywho, I think it's only fair to let the kid speak his truth. So, here's how the story goes: It was a summer day, the kind of day ... okay, I said that part. Moving on. It was such a day as this that Ryan and Pat's (his mother's) tires literally melted to the iron rod, blowing Pat's tires off the rims. They had been driving for almost fifty hours fleeing the Italian Mob, who would be most likely looking for Ryan's father, Connor O'Conner, who was a high-ranking member of the Irish Mob.

The Irish Mob was in too deep with the Italian Mob, who wanted them to close down the liquor stores in the community which they shared. But Ryan's father, all of six-foot-five, two hundred and ninety pounds, with a punch more powerful than Rocky's, told them freaking Italians that they would have their drinks all day every day if they so choose. In fact, Connor was so indignant at the request he *dared* the Italians to try and take away their drinks.

The Irish never tried to take spaghetti away from the Italians, by the way. Spaghetti is just as bad because it's high in carbs and when consumed in a large amount it will kill you (Ryan's story).

Anyway, the Italians had no right to even suggest something the Irish loved so much had to go. So, Connor O'Conner declared war and sent out the statement: "We will drink on the porches, in the parks, and in the restaurants" (Italian restaurants, no doubt), and begged them clowns to ride down on his Irishmen. Ryan's father's group was the Green Pride, and the Italian crew was the Meatball Thunder. Well, anyway, the Meatball Thunders told that Green Pride group that they would have their rumble, and the last man standing would be the best (and possibly the only) man standing.

Now, at this point in the story, I told Ryan it would be so cool if the two groups broke off into a song and dance, but he reminded me that he was, in fact, authoring this story, and he was telling the truth, the whole truth, and nothing but the truth, and everyone knows Irish don't dance. Now, I tried to remind him about the Irish stepdance, like the Riverdance, but you know what he said—his story, so let him tell it.

Well, anyway, the Green Pride was out for blood. The nerves of the Meatball Thunders to try and tell them they couldn't have their drinks! Getting drunk was a rite of passage and something the Green Pride had no problem with. (Remember, his story, I'm just telling you how it was told to me.)

So the night before all this was to go down, the menfolk made the womenfolk leave, never to return. "Never to return?" I questioned, and he reiterated, "Never to return." They gave each of them the wheels they needed to drive away with and a long, passionate kiss. They also gave them divorce papers and the right to change their names. Pat swore to Ryan's dad with tears in her eyes that she would never love another, never in her life.

This was really hard for Ryan to tell, because with his father losing his mother, he witnessed an Irishman cry. His father wept so loud and long the ground shook and the moon turned bright orange. When his dad stood back up after crying so long and hard, his eyes were bloodshot red, and his hair turned sliver. He had been transformed into an Irish god, and everyone knew this. He was ready to let his family go and fight for the honor of his community. It was the way that his father and mother loved that made his dad a hero in Ryan's eyes, not the fact that he was fighting for a community so that that community could stay drunk.

The duel was to take place that Friday night, and the women, children, and old people had to leave. In Pat's flight to get away, she knew she need to drive 120 on the expressway in the dead of the heat. Although she felt one of the wheels on the car was shaking, she had to get away; if the Italians ever found her, they would kill her and the son of god Connor O'Conner. If god Connor won the duel, a mark would be on his family because someone would take revenge, and if he lost the fight, the Italians would look high and low to get rid of this whole family, because if a son of a god grows up, he has to kill all of the Italians connected with that duel. It has to be done, that's just the way it is.

So, Pat leaving her husband and uprooting the family was the only respectable thing to do. Being in this position is very perplexing and complicated, especially if you have children. Pat knew she could not migrate to an area where she would fit in because they would know. I mean, the word travels like that—the son of a god is hard to hide. She knew she had to go and live amongst another race of people, so she asked Mother Mary for a sign, and right when she exited the expressway, her wheels melted off the rims right in front of a junky-looking garage, which just happens to fix cars. It's hard to believe that Mother Mary would send her there, but it was cheap, and Mother Mary slept in a barn to save money, so saving money is very important to Mother Mary.

Now, please understand I had to correct him on this; I wouldn't be a good Baptist if I didn't. I had to let the kids know that Joseph and Mary had to sleep in the barn because there was no room at the inn. We sing songs about this, we've done plays concerning this night, and not to mention, all of the nativity depicts this very scene. I just couldn't let him mess this part up. He silently agreed and proceeded to continue his story by saying that, when her wheels came off the rims, they stopped at what seemed to be a pitstop—a run-down raggedy-shabbily of a building, which was the mechanic's shop owned by big and very scary Bruce.

Now, remember, this was a hot day and an even hotter night. Ryan's mother was so distracted and tired, all she wanted was one drink of water. The lonely and sad mechanic's shop owner told her, "I will give you that drink if you will give me your heart." Now, according to Ryan, she accepted that offer, because if she didn't have water right that very minute, her son would probably have died. Afraid for her life and the life of her young son of Connor O' Conner—the god son—Pat gave her heart to the mechanic who gave her water. That very night, they sealed their love in the back seat of her car while Ryan ate a burger and fries.

Well, that's Ryan's story. Oh, and the reason he was at the Catholic school first is because he was at a Catholic school on the south side of Chicago, so all they had to do was transfer his records. If you attended one Catholic school you attended them all. I've come to learn there is no telling what Ryan won't say. He once told me his grandmother was secretly a nun, who secretly married a priest, and they raised together three whole kids in the convent. I know you are wondering: how did she deliver the babies? God did it, according to Ryan. At night with no help, the babies just popped out. It was a water-to-wine miracle.

See what I have to put up with? And no matter how we argue that this couldn't possibly be true, Ryan never changes his story because that is the kind of person Ryan is. Other than creating all these unbelievable hyperboles, if he had two cents, he would gladly give you one, and if you go down, he's got your back, and if he had to create a bigger lie to get out of a lie, if he likes you, he will do it. If Ryan liked you, you didn't have to earn it, and if he didn't like you, you didn't have to earn that either. Basically, it depends largely on what he ate the night before and how much it matters to you whether he likes you or not. To me, it mattered none, not even a little bit, so he liked me right from the start.

Now, my Uncle Bruce tells it a different way, so I guess it's fair to share his side of the story. He met Pat at his shop as she drove her beaten-up Ford to his mechanic's shop on two flat tires. He sort of felt sorry for her, a young lady trapped in the hood with two flat tires and very little money. He fixed her car and offered her leftover burgers. She refused his help and paid for the food. She also told him he was running his business all wrong and helped him sort of reorganize the place. She was a quiet thunderbolt with a heart of gold.

When he fixed her car, the two of them talked all night about so many things. She had left an abusive relationship, and he had just ended a relationship because his ex-girlfriend cheated on him. She offered to work for him on commission, and he accepted, and they simply liked each other. The race didn't even matter, especially when they each had someone they could simply laugh with. It took a while, and they didn't hook up overnight, but they grew to love each other and now they live above us in the three-bedroom apartment, and Pat is still the part-time secretary at the mechanic's shop. She works mornings for our school, St. Joseph's, and part-time in the mechanic's shop.

I liked Pat right off. She was so easy to convince and didn't always assume we shortiez were lying. She also just bonded with my mother; they are like sisters, getting up at 5 a.m. and going to the thrift stores, grocery stores, working out together, or staying up late at night cooking Thanksgiving dinner and listening to music, and don't even mention Christmas Eve — those two will be wrapping presents and wearing the same PJs, just like sisters.

When I first met Ryan, I didn't like or dislike him, he was just a weird kid with red hair. As I got to know Ryan, I realized he may feel left out (my mother could have dropped that in my ear). My mother thought he was a kid trying desperately to hold on to the little of his life he still had from before my uncle stole his mother's heart. Ryan would twirl his toy airplanes (homemade from hangers) and stare out the windows; you could tell he would rather be someplace else. Pat went out and bought him all the latest clothes, but nothing really moved him. Oddly, the only person he spoke to was crazy Grandpa. Ryan was like this superhero, afraid to fly.

At school, before Marion and Stinky came, he was just a punching bag for some of the kids. He wasn't ever afraid to stick up for himself, but he just never had anyone to pick him up when he fell down, and in the hood, someone will try you. One day, I decided I would be that person who picked him up (also, my mom told me it was the right thing to do). We really bonded when I overheard a conversation Ryan was having with Grandpa. I wanted to know all about this conversation, so I asked him, "Why do you talk to Grandpa, only?"

Ryan looked back at me, and it was at this point I realized he had nice green eyes. "Well," he said, melancholy, "he always wants me to get bananas for him, knowing it's going to make him fark."

"I know, right!" I enthusiastically agreed.

"So I just talk and lie to him all the time. He farks and I lie."

"Makes sense," I said.

Then Ryan let me in on one of his secrets. "I told him one day that I found a bag of money and I hid it in a blue garbage can somewhere on Iowa Street, the recyclable cans."

"We don't have blue garbage cans in the hood, Ryan."

"I know." Ryan smiled.

I thought Grandpa was upset because he couldn't find the money. Turns out, he was upset because he didn't see one damn blue garbage can.

I laughed. Not only because Ryan had figured out Granddad, which can be a challenge within itself, but because we were alike in so many ways; we had both inherited a family that we didn't understand, and we both were slowly coming to terms with the fact that maybe we won't ever understand, and maybe they are weird, crooky, odd-talking, farking, jerk-faced, and jewelry-thieving, but they are family nonetheless. As for Ryan, he didn't just become my friend that day; he became family.

5

☞

THE RAG-TAG CREW: WHO IS SHARIE?

Sister Mergie was the color of a copper penny; she wore a veil attached to a white coif. She was thin, but not too thin; her hair was long, but very kinky, and it hung stubbornly down her back almost to her buttocks, which made her look kind of funny because she was short, around five foot one. We all wondered, if her hair grew any longer, would she trip over it? Or grow so long that she would have to live in a tree and invite company to come up by climbing her incredibly long, coarse rope-hair? Oh, wait a minute, I think that story has already been written.

Anyway, Sister Mergie, who comes to us by way of Trinidad and Tobago, was a new addition to our school, and need I say, a welcome addition. She speaks English with a funny accent and a language known as Creole. Sister Mergie had invaded our space, and with her, close to her hip, were all her reasons for coming to this small Catholic school in a working poor African-American community, and she wasn't about to lose sight of her true calling.

I knew when I first laid eyes on her that she was the kind of person who held her reasons close. They were her prime motivation, similar to my father's Thanksgiving Day food list. Everything on that list he was going to make sure we had that year, even if he had to drive miles, fight in long superstore mall lines, or preach it out of you—needless to say, he was getting his divine meal, just like Sister Mergie was getting a group of kids who could barely speak English to speak sign language.

This nun did not talk much, and when she did talk, it sounded like she was talking through a baritone trumpet. Her speech was slow and exact, but the only really clear word we all understood was "no." I later learned that she was deaf or hard of hearing, but as she had hearing early on in life, she could understand sound, and she was an excellent lip and face reader.

Deaf people like to be referred to as hard of hearing. I didn't know that some deaf people hear inner ear sounds and they can actually feel vibrations. Sister Mergie explained that she hears with her heart and speaks with her hands; she was part of a pilot program with the goal of fostering the hard-of-hearing community in their own communities so that they will understand the cultural context of their same-age peers.

I know all this sounds complicated, and she didn't dumb it down for us. Some of us had to catch up. What I gather that she meant was that since hard-of-hearing kids have to be around the people in their community, they might as well learn how to communicate with the people in their community. Her goal was to work with the American Society for Deaf Children and create programs that bridged the two cultures.

Now, believe it or not, within four months, Sister Mergie had a group of misfits singing and signing Christian songs. A whole group of around one hundred hard-of-hearing kids came to see this, and in the crowd was Ms. Nelson and her princess-of-a-grandchild, Sharie.

It wasn't until that day that I came to understand why no one ever talked to Sharie. She was a Drake girl like me, same age, and we never ever spoke. When we had block parties, she would sit on the porch, dressed the best, and you knew you had better not approach her. Her hair was always in place, lips always glossy, nails always white; when she walked past you, if you were clear-headed, you just might bow, as if the princess was coming, but at the very least you'd get out of her way.

Ryan thought she was a life-sized doll, but I knew she was real, just a little different, and that day I found out why. Sharie was deaf. I was hear-hustling when I heard the conversation Ms. Nosy Nelson (as she is known in the community) was having with my mother. Apparently, public school wasn't working out for little Ms. Princess. The kids were picking on her and touching her hair. My mother introduced Ms. Nosy Nelson to Sister Mergie, and the rest is History. The next quarter, we had three new hard-of-hearing students, and the only one who lived on Drake Street was Sharie.

I remember when I was introduced to Ms. Sharie. She was polite—I thought a little too polite. She actually reached out and shook my hand. My mother looked down at Sharie with almost-tears in her eyes and said, "Poor girl, kids were actually hitting this poor little deaf child. Well, I tell you what, sweetheart. Had I seen it, I would have fought those girls myself!"

Then my mother turned her attention to Ms. Nelson, who was getting some weird sort of satisfaction from my mother's comforting words. But I caught it, even if my mother did not. I caught it. Maybe it was the gentle flicker of her long lashes or the way she threw her head back and smiled. Ms. Nelson wanted a full fill-up of sympathy, bowing her head in shame and holding back tears, but Sharie did not. In fact, it didn't appear that she wanted any at all. So I signed to Sharie, "I have a feeling the other kids needed to be protected from you."

"Damn straight," she signed back.

This is the day she became my bestie, my ride-or-die chick, my lunch meal ticket or late-night snacks or the clean house I could always go to when I wanted to get away from my lunatic brother. I liked her straightaway. We had a secret language code the rest of the world couldn't understand, and that bonded us.

Sharie is the kind of person who gives you information on a need-to-know basis. One day, we were walking home and we saw a little girl holding her father's hand, and that's when Sharie told me she had a little sister on her father's side, and her name was Hailey. I asked if she was hard of hearing, and she said no, and that was it. I met Sharie's mother around twice. She would come over and Sharie told me that they would have to lock all her stuff up until she left. She said her necklace was missing, but she wasn't sure her mother took it. She could have lost it.

She loved her mother, but her mother was sick and that's all she ever said about her. I did ask her one day about her father, and she didn't say anything, but about three weeks later, I was having dinner at her house and she signed, very casually, as if I had just asked her the question about her father that day, "My father is an ignorant dick."

I laughed because she had signed a bad word right at the dinner table, right in front of her grandmother.

Then she signed, "Look at all those clothes over there. They are probably all going to be too big."

"Just give him your size," I said.

"I do, all the time, but he doesn't know how to listen. All that stuff is probably stolen anyway."

"Why're you wilding out on your father like that?" I said.

"Know what he said to me?"

"What?" I asked curiously.

"He said to me that I'm going to have to stop using my hands and use the little words, just talk real slow."

I laughed, and Sharie couldn't help herself, she laughed, too.

"What did you say back to him?" I asked.

"Nothing. I wanted to show him exactly what he was going to get with my words, the dumbass."

We both laughed again, and this time, Ms. Nelson looked up from her plate of food. I had to tell her that we were excited about the food, as I didn't want her to think we were talking about her. So, Sharie and I did the table bet again over who can finish their greens the fastest, and this time she won.

There are lots of things I can say about my bestie: She likes to dance, and she dresses nicely. She's down for Drake Street and is never afraid to tell the truth, except when she wants to tell an untruth. We both have huge crushes on Mario Van Peebles and Michael Jackson. I think I can sing like Michael Jackson and Sharie thinks she can dance like him. I also liked Bruce Springsteen, but that's a secret I will take with me to my cold box of stone twelve feet under. The only person who knows this is Sharie, and she won't tell because she is really good at keeping secrets.

One thing you'd better know: Sharie does not like to be called "disabled." As she will tell you, she's able to do exactly what she wants to do, and she also doesn't like pity. I myself like pity, especially when I know I don't need it. All in all, we are not joined at the hip as most people would like to think, but we are certainly two peas in the same pot.

6

THE RAG-TAG CREW: WHO ARE MARION AND STINKY?

There are days when everything is low in the hood. You don't hear the loud noises bumping from the trunks of cars, or speakers blaring, or dogs barking through black gates. You don't see many people walking down the street—a few here and there, but not many. People sit on porches or red crates with lazy glares as if they just missed something and forgot what it is they missed. The hood aroma is turned down, so you don't smell the scent of soul food taunting and teasing your taste buds—a smell strong enough to invite your memory back to fatback in greens, fried chicken, honey-baked hams, yams covered in brown sugar, three-layer baked mac and cheese, cornbread, or butter-and-honey-covered biscuits.

You don't get any of that goodness on turned-down days; smells, music, voices, and even moving feet sound like they're turned on low. Life sort of creeps on by, for life has lived in the reality of movement, anxiety, and worry for most of the week, but on turned-down days, life sort of gives the people a vacation from giving and taking, thinking and wanting, and for maybe just moments, people just exist without any care of knowing.

If you are lucky, you realize that days like these are a blessing from God; if you are foolish, you long for these days to end so that you can get back to the busyness of event planning.

I never wanted these days to end, for these days may be the few times in my hood I can hear thoughts—including my own. These low days usually come to us on Saturday mornings, and they rarely last past noon.

On this particular Saturday, Sharie and I were sitting on our porch. No need to do much on low days. Ryan was in the house doing homework which he would, of course, forget to bring back to school on Mondays. I felt like walking because I knew Sharie had money (and, of course, I didn't), and I also knew she would buy me a little treat, a Push-Up ice cream bar or something sweet.

So, in the laziness of the day I asked her, "Hey, you wanna walk to the store?"

Sharie looked in her purse, pulled up ten dollars, and signed, "Sure, why not."

So, we did, and the day was going all so well when this strange image presented itself to us.

When we got to the corner, about to go into the store, we saw it. We just stopped and looked. It was hard to believe what we were seeing, but we were both seeing it. Could it be a turned-down day trick of our imaginations? We walked closer just to check it out, and there it was: Ms. Nelson, Sharie's very own grandmother, was talking to Rosetta.

This was a really big deal, like Channel 7 News big. You see, no one talked to the New York immigrant, Rosetta, except maybe my mother. Even if you talked to her, you probably wouldn't understand much. Her mouth moved and words came out very strangely. In that dialect of hers, her consonants were all oversimplified and her vowels were extended. But there were other reasons we didn't talk to this New York princess. The truth of the matter is, she was the envy of the hood, but people wouldn't let her know this, so people just simply avoided her—for her sake, of course. They didn't want pride to give her a big head.

In the eyes of the young girls that shyly looked up to this strange New York plant, she was the Sugar, Honey, Iced Tea, an oversized bag of chips with dip, and bad "A" hair whip on the side. She was the hood's Kim Kardashian. She had body piercings and a small diamond nose ring, and this was unheard of until she came to the hood. People wouldn't dare tell this plant she inspired them with her piercings, but if you just look around, everybody but church women has got 'em now. Her nails were long and glossy, with acrylic tips. Now, almost everyone's got long nails that they can do very little with, but those nails look like Hollywood and they make the common girls feel sophisticated, so thanks again, New York.

Rosetta's skin glowed chestnut brown, and her lips were so glossy that it always looked like she'd just completed a bucket of chicken by herself. If you ever caught her smiling, you witnessed how perfectly straight and white her teeth were, complemented by deep dimples that sort of relaxed her face. But what really made her both an admirable and contemptible member of our hood is what we watched when she walked past or stood still.

She was all of five foot four, and if she had a waistline, you didn't see it. Could be you didn't see it because you were distracted by the breasts that protruded from the front and the huge butt that hung from the back. Her butt looked like someone had blown up two large balloons, filled them with water, then placed them perfectly below her lower back.

She walked much differently from the women in my hood, which made her stand out even more. She walked like she was sweeping the floor with her hips, slowly, from side to side. Most women in my hood just walked to get from place to place, but when she walked, her presence drew your attention, and you knew you were watching a person who knew where her steps were taking her. You can imagine the thoughts people had when they saw her coming, sweeping the earth from side to side. So, what is it that people did when she walked near? Well, what do people do when you sweep? That's right, they move out of the way.

How did New York get to Chicago, you ask? It was said that Sam moved her here because he was changing the base of his operation to Chicago. Who's Sam? He was a hood pharmacist, gang banger, and leader of all things tough and bad. He was a mysterious man himself, that Sam. People said nothing to him and nothing about him because they didn't want to wake up dead the next morning. If Sam didn't shoot you, Rosetta just might.

Two boys moved with Rosetta from New York. The oldest one was quieter but loved sports. You mostly saw him with a football or basketball. The youngest one was loud and boastful, and most people called him "Stinky" because he smelled like pee. He was bold and he knew everybody. I never told him my name, but he knew it. He was a little more familiar with Ryan, always asking him, "Who moved you on my block?" as if white people couldn't live on Drake.

Needless to say, I didn't like the kid much, but he was a Drake boy. His mother, Ms. Rosetta, was tough in a nice way. One day, Stinky threw his ball into the yard of a neighbor who had dogs in the backyard. Rosetta was trying to get the neighbor's attention because Stinky was crying—he wanted his ball. The neighbor wouldn't come to the window or door, and that Miss New York started threatening to shoot the dogs. She used so many vulgarities … it was bad. Really bad. In fact, that's how my mother and Ms. New York sort of became friends.

My mother stopped her from shooting the dogs. She called the neighbor on the phone, and they came right out and gave Stinky his ball back. Think Ms. New York was grateful? Well, think again. She told that neighbor that next time, she was going to shoot the dogs. She was glad my mother helped, though. The next day, she gave my mother really hot sausages in brown rice with carrots and lots of other indescribable food products. It was a colorful mess.

You see, Ms. New York was always making treats, dishes with food products that should never be paired together, like baked potatoes and beets, or steak with caramel sauce. That steak was very sweet, but not half bad. Sometimes she gets it right, but most times it's just bad. That time, my mother thanked her and threw it out. But anyway, that's why she talks to my mother.

The day after the whole thing with the dogs, Sam told that neighbor to move those dogs to the garage and said they could only be brought out when the kids were at school, and, of course, the neighbor complied. They didn't want to wake up dead the next morning.

Stinky's father was the hood's international hoodlum. There are stories written about this man in invisible ink. My brother and I were forbidden to say anything to him; when he walked past us, we were all told to look down, no eye contact. He was just the type of man you didn't want to tangle with, my father said.

Strangely enough, it didn't seem to bother him that no one talked much to him except his crew. I guess he had lots of friends because he always had gangs of boys with him, and I guess they reported everything back to him because he knew everyone's name and the family they belonged to, come to think of it. That could be how Stinky got all that information. On those rare occasions when he saw us kids doing something we weren't supposed to do, he told us to go home before he told our parents.

He caught me saying an unsavory word one day—not that I'm proud of this, but it happened. He told me he didn't think church girls talked like that. I was embarrassed and honored at the same time. He knew exactly who I was. Now I guess he won't know much of anything because he is in jail. There was this shootout that left one man dead on the avenue. According to the hood, even though Sam wasn't there doing the murder, he certainly went to jail for it. So, while he is fighting this case, he has Ms. New York running the hood.

So, when I say we saw her talking to Ms. Nelson, we were, of course, taken aback. I've never seen Rosetta with a gun, but they say she always carries one. I don't know if this is true, but what I do know is that Rosetta and Sam have the best-looking two flat on our block, and the only two flat with only one family living in it, a gold fence protecting it, cameras all around it, and floodlights that would light up an outdoor movie set. It has also been said that a tunnel under their apartment leads all the way back to New York.

Again, you can imagine our surprise when we saw this little New York talking to the gossip of the community. We got a little closer—so close that Ms. Nelson had to acknowledge us. We spoke and she smiled. She was telling Ms. Nelson about the school wanting to put Stinky in a kind of special class, and Ms. Nelson was telling her about our school. She was going on and on about how glad she was that she got Sharie out of that public school. I wondered how much Ms. New York was actually listening. She told her about the small classroom sizes, hard-of-hearing programs, hot lunches, and teachers. She just went on and on and on.

The next week, there were two new boys in our school. At first, we still didn't know them, we still didn't have much to say to them, but we all walked the same way home.

As life would have it, a week or so later, there was this really big kid picking on Stinky, calling him these really bad names. What did he call him? Oh yeah, it was "stink-bum." Stinky was a short kid, but he was a fearless kid. He told the boy to say it again, and, of course, the big kid said it again, but this time, Stinky hit that big kid.

Sharie told me the little kid actually stood up for her one day in public school. I guess it was because they lived on the same block. Well, anyway, this big kid was picking Stinky up off his feet, getting ready to drop him to the concrete, when out of the blue, Ryan gave this kid a gut punch, landing him and Stinky on the ground. Now, this is how Sharie and I got into the mix, because this kid was slowly standing up, and truthfully we didn't think Ryan had a chance. As luck would have it, when he finally made it to his feet, he had Marion to deal with, and although Marion was only in the sixth grade, this kid had nothing on him. Come to think of it, this was how Marion got the name "Hands."

While Sharie and I were running to give Ryan and Stinky help, we didn't have much to do because Marion gave that big kid so many blows you would have thought he was the Rock 'Em Sock 'Em robot toy. Needless to say, we all ended up in detention the next day, and after detention we all walked home. Ryan invited Marion and Stinky to our clubhouse, and we all sort of became friends.

Well, I am not a big fan of Stinky. He talks too much, and out of the blue the kid will drop the F-bomb. He even did it in chapel. He was the candle boy, and he almost dropped the long candlestick, and out of his mouth came so many F-words you would have thought he was getting paid to drop the F-bomb. We all laughed, and throughout chapel we all passed the F-word around like a collection plate. Marion said we were F-ing going to go to hell for that.

Well, we didn't go to hell, but we did earn a trip to the principal's office. We all ended up in detention for that, too. As for Stinky, he was ushered to the back room and prayed for, or given ice cream, or offered a towel to wash up with, or something like that. Whatever he got, it was not a punishment.

Well, I guess that's how the rag-tag group got together. Like I said, we are not joined at the hip, just connected because we all live on Drake Street, and we all just happen to be some really cool kids who've got each other's backs—that you'd best believe!

7

THE LONG WALK HOME

I was on my way home, and due to recent events, I would rather be going anywhere but home. To escape the fate that awaited me, my mind began to wander, and the only thing I could think about was this: Why is hair such a big deal anyway? Why must I even have to explain to my mother that she will have to take down this fresh hairdo, and wash it, and have it re-braided? Why couldn't I just wear the messed-up braids? Well, I'll tell you why—because I got sand in it.

Okay, you don't get it, but let's just put it this way: sand and African-American hair is disastrous. That's why you don't see black people at the beach, the sand takes out our hair. If someone got sand in their hair, it was a national crisis in the hood. You had to quickly comb out the hair, wash it twice, and, of course, wear that ridiculous conditioning cap much longer than usual lest you deal with being bald-headed. That's what happened to Mrs. Smith's hair. She ain't got no hair around her edges because she didn't wash out the sand soon enough.

The only thing that would distract my mother from the sand in my hair would be a Daddy good day. I found myself wishing and praying that Daddy would do good today. If Dad would have a reason to surprise my mother with something special, sand in my hair wouldn't be a problem. It would be like the time when Daddy brought home candy just because. My mother smiled almost the whole day. I had lost my key to the house, but it didn't matter. She just gave me the spare key and told me to be careful.

Yeah, that happened. I tell you, she didn't even lecture me about being more responsible. Boy, I hoped this was one of those days. If it was, maybe I wouldn't get in trouble for getting a last-chance write-up. There was something in the pit of my gut that told me I was going to meet *"Papa can't save you now"* Mama.

My punishment? I would be locked in my room for around ten years, and my only visitor would be my grandad, who would come not to comfort me, but to confuse me or make matters worse. He's a funny fart, that man is, and he gives terrible advice.

Then again, she might let me out around my eighteenth birthday. By that time, she would have hoped I'd met and married common sense, so I wouldn't get in trouble all the time and wouldn't let anyone put sand in my hair. I really didn't know which one was worse, the sand in my hair or the write-up. All I knew was that they were both bad.

We walked and Stinky talked. He was still trying to figure out who could have taken that picture. Then he stopped, and we stopped, as he announced, "I got it! I know who took that picture!"

"Who?" I asked. Not that I really wanted to know—in fact, I already knew, and, really, I think we all knew other than Stinky—but he had been really deep in thought over this.

Then he announced with confidence, "Well, I think it was Sharie's grandma!"

Sharie snapped back, "Well, I think it was yo mama!"

"No, hear me out, Sharie. Who likes to take pictures?" Stinky asked

"Yo mama!" Sharie declared.

"Who cares who took the picture?" I interjected.

Really, I just wanted Stinky to get off Sharie, because he was right. Ms. Nelson most certainly did that. But Sharie should not be held accountable for the actions of Ms. Nosey Nelson (as she's affectionately known in the hood).

"She ain't gonna keep talking about my mama," said an agitated Stinky.

Stinky was mad, but he gives Sharie grace he wouldn't give to the rest of us. Had we said that about him, we would have gotten the F-word up, down, and sideways. But honestly, Sharie is a little nicer to Stinky, so he likes her a little more and takes a little back talk from her. Had that been me, though …

We all walked on silently, not daring to say we all sort of thought it could have been Sharie's grandmother. She's always keeping an eye out on us. I guess she must think we're a bad influence on Sharie, but the truth of the matter is, her granddaughter, even though she's mute, is just another shortie from the hood; she's no different from the rest of us.

When we walked the long way home, we really walked *the long way* home. I only hoped my dear mother was cooking so she would be too tired to fuss and that we would be right on time for dinner. I figured if we were on time, we just might be allowed to eat first, and sometimes food energizes your thoughts. We could possibly even come up with a totally new refreshing twist to our story, one that would make all of us look like heroes.

Besides, I'd gotten most of the white stuff out of my hair. It was still frizzy-looking, but at least I didn't look like a gray-headed old lady.

"There go those shadows again," Ryan said very nonchalantly.

The shadows are our lookalikes—strange, but lots of strange things happen in my hood. Mr. Reynolds takes out his teeth, both top and bottom, right out of his mouth, and those teeth outside his mouth talk to you like a puppet or something. You don't see his mouth moving. He just folds his bottom and top lips together and those teeth just keep talking. He always says you can't tell him to shut up if he is not moving his mouth. Lots of people find it funny, but as for me, I just find it strange.

The unusual is common around here, and besides, maybe there aren't any shadow people following us. Lots of the time, we eat greasy food. My grandpa always says that if you eat greasy foods, your imagination can run away from you. I have always taken "your imagination running away" to simply mean you will start seeing illusions. That could be what was happening with us. Our imaginations were simply running away from us and we were delusional. So, in our state of sheer confusion, we all saw shadow people that looked like us. Yeah, that was it.

Then again, as I thought more about it, I considered what may be a more logical choice: it could very well be the trees reflecting on the ground that look just like the five of us. Whatever it is, it has been happening for about two weeks or so. It's like we are being followed by *us*. Strange and weird, but that's why I don't think about it much.

One day, these shadow people were on the side of the bus, waving goodbye to us. Stinky waved back. We mostly see them when we are together, but I saw them on the back of the church building; they looked to be smiling. That particular time, Shadow Marion had his hair in braids, and when I saw him later that day, guess what? He had his hair in braids.

I wanted to tell someone or do a little logical research to see what this phenomenon could be, but I didn't, and that's strange because I like doing research and I love reading. But somehow, when I got around adults or books, I simply forgot about it.

Then they would appear again—normally when we were outside playing or just chilling in the clubhouse. Sharie noticed them on the ground at the playground. They were right in front of us, and the sun was shining, and it was becoming a little too normal for me.

Stinky just said, "Those shadows again, right in front of us. "

Marion interjected. "I keep telling you, clown, shadows can't be in the front. It can only be a shadow if it's in the back of you. Got that?"

"Yeah," said Stinky.

He seemed a little unsure as to why he agreed with his big brother. It was kind of hard to take Marion seriously when there the shadows were, waving at us. He, too, was looking at the floor shadows, and all he could do was swallow hard and close his eyes as if to wish them away, but they didn't go anywhere.

"Whatever it is, it's us. The shadows are us. Look at your hair." I pointed to Ryan's spike hair on the shadow, and everyone laughed.

"Look, it's going behind the Oscar Mayer factory," Sharie signed.

"Let's follow," I said.

As we walked behind the Oscar Mayer factory, we noticed the shadows facing us were waving hi. Or at least, it looked like the shadows on the wall were waving hi. We all walked closer to the shadows. Why we were putting one foot in front of the other, as if we were babies just learning how to walk, I didn't know.

The closer we got to the shadows, the more we stooped low to the ground, as if we didn't want the shadows to see us coming.

I just know that I wanted to laugh for some strange reason. It had to be a joke. It was mid-day, not night, and we saw shadows in the front of us, not the back, and they were exact replicas of us plastered to a wall in the back of an old factory, waving at us. And like we ain't got nothing better to do, there we were, walking closer to them.

I don't think we even knew why we were walking toward a wall. It was clear these figures on the wall couldn't talk. If they could talk, what would we say to ourselves? I had another thought: I bet this must be some sort of television show my grandfather volunteered us for. The old fart was capable of doing anything.

Just when I was convinced in my own mind that it was time to go home, face the music, and leave this nonsense alone, Stinky, on sheer impulse, ran to the wall, jumped, and gave his shadow a high-five. At that very moment, a bright, colorful light illuminated the factory's wall, and then — SWOOSH — we were all sucked into a vacuum.

It felt like our stomachs were being filled with air, and suddenly, I had the need to pee. We were being pulled upward — upward like a quiet but swift elevator ride with no music. My mind was going through an array of colors as the glass box of the elevator was appearing to get smaller.

As we were reaching what I assumed to be the top floor, our clothes started to mysteriously change. I was wearing a beautiful new pink outfit with a new pair of pink shoes. My hair was being straightened out, then curled — it felt like electricity was going through my hair. I looked over at Sharie, and she had on a white dress with sneakers — very tasteful sneakers — and the boys all had on flashy designer clothes with the latest sneakers. *My imagination makeover*, I thought. Then I preferred to think nothing at all.

The fall forward actually felt enjoyable. I could feel the air slowly escaping my body, I was becoming lighter. Then, all of a sudden, I felt a wave of joy flood my body, like when you taste your favorite dessert for the first time. *This is lovely, just lovely*, I thought. When had anything been "lovely" in my life? It's not a word I would use, but seeing as this was my imagination makeover, lovely was the word I used, and I stand by it. I looked lovely.

I heard the sound of clinking as accessories were being added. I had a tasteful white pearl necklace and earrings. My hair was now permed straight, and it dropped down my back. That also excited me! I'd had shoulder-length hair before, but now my hair was down my back. Cool. The new me was really cool.

As I looked around at my friends, I noticed they were having their own experiences. We each had on clothes I knew we could not have afforded in our hood. It was a welcome and much-needed makeover. I'd always wanted a pink dress just like this, and now I had it on.

We landed in a place that looked like a lost island: white sand and beautiful blue waters like Crater Lake in Oregon. Had I ever been there? Of course not, but I loved to read and learn fun facts, which was often all I could do when I was on punishment (which had been happening much too often lately).

Something about that place held a tight grip on stillness. Nothing moved but our imaginations, and, at times, Stinky's pantlegs. The air was so light that birds didn't have to flap their wings to fly—they just sort of glided through the air, as if they were curious about the wonder of this place as well. The rocks along the coast formed a beautiful stone wall. I looked at Marion and could imagine what he was thinking, as we all were thinking it: all we needed was a can of spray paint, and we could tag up that wall.

A bird flew quickly above our heads. It sounded as if it were singing. Yes, *singing*. Like a lullaby. Now I know where people get the phrase "sing like a bird" from. I tell you, that always confused me because where I come from, birds didn't sing. If you asked me, all birds ever did was chirp and drop white poop all over the place. Suddenly, I wondered, where were the people? Who else lived here to witness this astonishment?

Inside the sand were small pieces of white diamonds. There were several stools made out of stone but outlined in rubies and sapphires. A little further down on the white diamond-covered beach were marble chairs and one table. The sky was turning aquamarine, and the light purple moon was slowly emerging, so it wasn't really dark out, but it wasn't light, either. It was where I bet they got the word "dusk."

A purple moon! I thought. *I hope the rain isn't fire! OK, that's negative. Everyone else is enjoying this experience and so will I.*

It was as if we couldn't speak — too amazed to even look at each other. At that moment, another miracle happened. *Sharie* spoke.

"Where are we?"

Hearing her voice, she held her ears and fell to the ground. She twirled around as if the sound was absorbing her. She touched the sand and made us each say the word "sand" like five times. Her words were slow but articulate. Words and sounds were coming from her mouth — this astounded her. Sharie had always wanted words to fall from her lips that didn't have to be caught with her imagination. They were real words, and it was beautiful!

For around thirty minutes or more we simply repeated words to her and watched as she took pleasure in hearing them, digesting each sound as if they were all delicate meals. With childlike joy, I watched my friend jump around, sometimes covering her eyes, exploring this world of words.

But that wasn't all. Stinky didn't stink anymore, and he was dressed in a fly blue jean suit. Ryan matched Stinky, except that his pants were white. Marion had fresh braids, an all-black suit, and a white leather jacket. He looked nice — not *"I like you, Marion"* nice, but just mature ... and *oh yeah* nice.

And, of course, I no longer felt like I needed to wash my hair, as it looked freshly done.

It was wonderful. Incredible. We had all transformed to flawless human beings. But the biggest wonder of all was hearing Sharie speak. In our surprise and disbelief, we kept asking Sharie questions, getting her to say more. Then, for a moment, Sharie stopped. She squinted, and we turned to look where she was looking.

Walking toward us was a tall, perfectly brown-tanned man wearing a white suit with a blue shirt. His black hair had a wet, slick look to it, and he had it pulled back into one long ponytail. He was smiling and waving at us. Everyone waved back, except me.

"Is that Principal Morten?" Sharie asked plainly.

As the strange image approached us, Sharie could only ask if her words sounded normal. I nodded yes, adding that, as this handsome figure of a man came nearer, only in Principal Morten's dreams could this man be him.

"I wonder who he is?" Sharie asked.

Sharie was talking, and we were still taking in that fact as the man came closer. Was he taking his time on purpose, so as not to interrupt our newfound joy?

At last, the man was in our presence, and we all pretty much had the same question for him.

"Where are we?" we demanded.

He smiled, and we felt at ease. He had a calming presence and we didn't feel afraid.

"Don't you want to know my name first?" he asked.

"Okay, what's your name?" asked Sharie.

"Well, Sharie, my name is Gill, and you are in Learned Kansan. There's no place like it in Middle Heaven."

I suddenly became sad, because if we were in heaven, that meant we'd died, and if we'd died, how had Stinky ended up in heaven? So, I had to ask him.

"Are we dead?"

The man laughed so hard he fell to his knees.

"No, you are in Learned Kansan. Most people just come here right from I-80, but you somehow got to us from the walls. Thought we had closed all that up. Anyway, consider this to be a vacation. You are officially the guests of Learned Kansan. No place like it on Earth. Would you like to know why?"

"Yeah, tell me why," Stinky demanded in a cocky manner.

"Well, little fellow, it's the only place on Earth where you can have whatever you say. If you say it, it appears!"

Stinky looked at him in total disbelief. "Oh yeah?" he finally said. "Well then, I want a chocolate sundae with a cherry on top." A few seconds later, some teenager on wheels with a chocolate sundae on a tray rolled up, presented it to Stinky, and left.

"It's a miracle," Stinky said, shocked and excited.

"Just like I said, young man, no place like it!" Gill confirmed. "Why don't you just relax and have fun? This is home now. Only a few choice people get to have a free break here."

Relax and have fun? How could we possibly relax? We were on an island—or whatever the place was—with curious kids who, by sheer luck, could have whatever they spoke. At that moment, the thought occurred to me that I could be having a silly nightmare or a dream. I could have been dreaming this all up to prevent the punishment that awaited me at home. So, if it was a dream and not a nightmare (after all, I hadn't seen any monsters yet), I figured I might as well enjoy it, right?

I shouldn't overthink. That's what everyone always told me, that I thought too much. But I sat on the sand and thought, *What have we gotten ourselves into now?*

8

GETTING TO KNOW STRANGE

Gill, our tour guide, took us around this magical town we had mysteriously appeared in and introduced us to quite a few people. They didn't appear abnormal at all. I was waiting for scary, but they weren't scary. It was more like, *"Hey a few kids from the wall! Oh, good to see y'all!"*

We also saw cows. I had eaten many of them before, but to be actually looking one in the face? That didn't happen often. Only at the zoo. I'd never been to a place where cows walked the streets like people, but apparently, this was normal in Learned Kansan farm life.

I could have sworn one of the cows smiled at me—I mean a big smile. Had I said this out loud, I am sure I would have been taken away to some strange nuthouse. However, this was life in Learned Kansan. That's how they're makin' a livin' round those parts, at least that's what I'm told. I guess there are worse ways to make a livin'.

My uncle bootlegs DVDs when he's not trying to fix cars, so maybe he would better understand the packing and selling of meat. We took a tour of how meat was prepared, and the foul odor in the place attached itself to our clothes. After that, I thought, *OK, now I can be a vegetarian.* I don't think you can watch the meat being prepared and still eat meat. Well, I didn't think that you could until I watched Marion, Stinky, and Ryan wolf down steak right after the tour. *Those boys — such barbarians*, I thought — until Sharie joined them. Then I just thought, *My friends are crazy.*

Later that evening, we went to the supermarket's deli and had corned beef sandwiches. I guess I just had to eat that corned beef, which caressed my taste buds and sent me to food heaven temporarily. I washed it down with watermelon soda. I'd never heard of watermelon soda before because I invented it, on the spot. I just said it and it appeared and that was cool. But this place? Not so cool at all.

It was the smell, I think. Things were too perfumed. When the wind blew, it felt like a fan. Why do I say this? When the wind blows at home, my eyes don't burn, but here, my eyes burned just a little, as they do when I am lying directly under a fan at home. Also, everything looked a little too perfect, and again, just not cool.

Gill showed us that we could fly and when we each spoke the words, "Man, it would be cool to fly!" off we went, cruising the skies with wonder and awe. That *was* really cool. We saw a small group of people buying movie tickets and kids enjoying themselves at an outdoor drive-in called "Shaker," eating slushy ice melts. We saw downtown Learned Kansan, which consisted of a courthouse and a couple of two-story business buildings.

This place was boring and exciting all at the same time. I wanted to just drench myself in the moment as my friends were doing, but somebody had to be level-headed to think of that question — that big question that no one else was forcing themselves to think.

"Wow! This place sure don't have many people like *us*." And what did I mean by this statement, you ask? Ain't too many black people in Learned Kansan, and the few that're there don't look like they know one thing about being black.

That place didn't seem to know what it was like to have a Black History Month program at church where Mr. Matin stands up and tells everyone that everything in the world came from black people — well, maybe not everything, but the cotton and all that sort of stuff. And Mr. Luis always makes sure he asks us one trivial question, and that is, "Who invented American Music?" and we all say "black people," and he slaps his shaking knee and laughs unrestrained, like he didn't expect us to know the answer when he's only told us a hundred times that the only music native to America is African American music, better known as blues. And let's not forgot Ms. Lane telling us in church that we are like the Hebrews, and that we can't allow slavery to define us because we're not a disenchanted group of hoodlums, but rather, the Chosen People.

They didn't seem to get that in Learned Kansan. Which was why we couldn't stay there. Fun? Yes, it was. But normal? No, it wasn't. Like, no black girls in my hood wear shorts that short, and their mamas wouldn't let them walk about in a swimsuit top ... I'm just sayin'. On a more positive note, I guess now we finally knew how Ryan must have felt all those years being the only white kid around all us black kids.

Stinky, who I am sure has limited mental resources, said to Ryan naively, "Think you got family members living here, Ryan."

"I don't think so," Ryan answered. "Why would you say something like that anyway?" We all looked at Ryan, for surely he must know ... but wait a minute, this was Ryan. He didn't have a clue, and none of us cared to explain it, so we let him stay clueless about that little connection.

Before we landed back on solid ground, Gill gave us one of the best toasted cheese sandwiches I had ever tasted — apparently one of the things people are known for in Learned Kansan. I'd always thought Wisconsin was the cheese state, but I wasn't about to argue with Gill. He was warm and gentle and everything seemed to excite him, just as it did us. We watched as children played with their parents on slides and in sandboxes. It was so peaceful it was almost mesmerizing. No one yelled. They simply sat and played.

I wasn't sure if the kids enjoyed it at all, though. It was as if they were just doing what was expected of them. Sort of like what happens when you get behind the wheel of a car and it just drives. OK, Ryan would have gotten *that* — no pun intended. I laughed at myself. *If I wasn't so intense, I might even enjoy this place.*

I guess what I really felt — and this was a scary thought — but it felt like, in this wonderland, people existed for one purpose. In fact, this whole little town felt as if it were sort of planted there to serve the same purpose. The guys at the car wash seemed fake—they wanted to shine their cars up just to drive around a place I am sure they had seen hundreds of times before. But the upkeep of the cars was real.

The cook at the small diner—fake. He smiled as if he had seen a ghost; it was like he was scared and fascinated by us at the same time. And as much as I liked our tall, tan, model-looking tour guide, he was, of course, in my mind, fake. I didn't know if it was the fake parents playing lovingly with their fake kids, or the fact that I was no longer entertained, but I felt it was time to ask what all my nincompoop friends seemed to have forgotten to ask about.

And so, I looked at all my nicely dressed fake friends and asked, "OK, when do we get to go back home? Let me have it. I've done all I wanna do."

Gill almost choked on his cheese sandwich. I could tell my question caught him off guard, as he must have thought the joy and fun would somehow cause us to forget about home. Yes, I have a home, and so do the rest of them: I live on Drake with my mama and father, big brother, and grandfather living on the first floor. My uncle and his girl, who is Ryan's mother, live on the second floor. I live one house over from Sharie, who grew up with me. My grandfather and her grandmother grew up together, they just don't like each other now, and I live one block over from Stinky and Marion, whose mother has the *bomb* of a shape — well, that's what everyone says.

OK, maybe home was not picture-perfect. But reality had set in for me, and I was hoping it was beginning to set in for everyone else as well.

"Oh, don't worry about those matters. You have only five days in this place, so enjoy it! You get to experience what is now considered a lost art — the joy of living in Middle Heaven."

"I don't want to live in Middle Heaven," I argued. "When I die, I would rather just go straight to Heaven, the real thing. So, shine the way back to Chicago, please."

Then Ryan turned around, and if I hadn't heard it for myself, I wouldn't have believed it. "Why you always get to say what happens? I, for one, want to be here for the five days. I mean, what we rushing back to Chicago for? Y'all know we weren't going to complete that task of ten good deeds, so why we rushing back to Chicago just to be in detention all summer?"

Stinky went and stood next to Ryan, which did not surprise me, as the mutiny officially formed. "Yeah," said Stinky, "who made you the boss of everything? You ain't the boss of me, and I want to stay. We get back when we get back."

Marion stood up and sided with his brother. *Wait a minute, I thought we were cool. What's happening in this world? Could it be that I'm the nobody here?* I was the boss back home, just like my granny. The big fish in a little pond or something like that.

Then, it happened—the straw that crushed the camel, then turned, buried the llamas, and blinded the alpacas. That straw that was my very best friend since the age of eleven, who taught me sign language so we could sit around adults and say bad words and laugh and no one would know what we were talking about, so we could share secrets, and crushes, and likes and dislikes, and answers to tests and quizzes when we got stuck, so we could share dreams we had with each other, us against the world—*my Sharie* had the nerves to say, "Salle, you cool and all and don't take it personally, but why are we rushing back?"

"No, Sharie, you got this all mixed up. The real question is, why don't you be a real friend and stay on my side?"

Everyone sided with Ryan and with Stinky — the same boy who sleeps in his clothes, pees his pants, and gets up and comes to school wearing those same clothes. They were all siding with that kid.

After carefully evaluating the situation, I decided to let the boys be boys. They could stay in this middle-of-nowhere place, and Sharie, she could stay too, but as for me, Salle with the E, I was going back home, the sensible thing to do.

"OK, you dumb bunnies," I said, "stay in no man's world. Sharie, you sure you want to side with *them* three? Think carefully—*I'm* going back!" I spoke confidently, waiting for Sharie's response. Usually, when I was adamant about a thing, Sharie would side with me, as she knew I was not often wrong.

Sharie said it rather boldly, not in sign language, so I'm sure I heard her right: "I'm staying."

What was happening in this place? I was losing my control, but I told myself to pull it together, that this was just a minor setback. Then Sharie added, "I sort of like hearing about new things, and I'd like to experience some more things before going back home."

"That so?" I said sarcastically.

"Yeah, that's so!" Sharie almost shouted back. She was standing her ground and wanted me to know she meant business.

I felt momentarily defeated, but only for a moment. I would just have to go home by myself. Gill stood with the four other clowns, a look of sheer delight on his face. He had accomplished his mission for the day, I am sure of that, but what he didn't know was that I now had outright contempt for him. I had one goal, and that was to find my way home, go get our parents, and let them raise the roof in this place. *So, say goodbye to Middle Heaven, you weirdos,* I thought to myself.

As if he could read my mind, Gill smiled and said, "One thing about Middle Heaven is that if one person stays, you all must stay. Might as well get comfy, young lady. Looks like this is home for you for now."

"I am leaving these clowns here; I know how to get back."

"That wall you got in will only light up if all of you are together, so you, Salle, are going to have to stay and have fun. Just know when you get back, it will be the same time and the same place. Come on, kiddo, what do you say?"

My silence was my defiance. I would not let Gill know he had, in fact, beat me with the full betrayal of all my friends. He waited until it felt too uncomfortable, then he announced, "So kids, here is the fun part, you get to do whatever you want to do, so what's your wildest dream?"

Ryan, excited, told Gill his ridiculous dream, and instead of us all laughing, it was now plausible. "I want to be a rapper, a rich rapper!"

Stinky added, "I'll be his sidekick. You know, like Flavor Flav — *Yeaaaah Booooy*." My eyes couldn't take looking at Stinky jumping around like a lost little monkey, giving everyone high fives.

"I would love to be the bodyguard, kick a few butts, and be adored by all the women — you know, like a stud or jock," said Marion.

You'll be a jock alright — more like a joke, I thought. Then I realized he'd always wanted to be good at sports for some reason. Now I knew why. However, he was good with his hands, but I had a feeling that wasn't important to him now.

"I know what you mean," added Sharie. "I would love to know what it would feel like to have a really nice-looking boyfriend" — she laughed — "that would listen to me talk all the time? Someone focused just on me for once?"

For once? I thought. *I do nothing but listen to those hands flap.*

As if I were watching a short-order cook, the requests came in. First, a young African American boy who looked like he'd stolen Will Smith's face jumped out of a limousine wearing dark shades. He approached Ryan and said, as if he were a door-to-door carpet salesman, "Ryan, you the hottest thing coming, and I am your manager."

"You are? I mean, I am the hottest thing coming?"

The manager continued in his carpet salesman's voice, "You are, kid! Trust me. We got to get you to the studio and on wax fast, 'cause the world is waiting to hear from you. But 'Ryan' is a little too bland, you too cool for that name." The sound of his cell phone ringing interrupted the bull he was selling Ryan.

"You're not going to believe this, kid, but we just booked you at the Coliseum. As I was saying, we can't call you Ryan, though. Not really a rap name, know what I mean? So, today you will be *Rain Man*, 'cause you know how to make it rain. And you, young man, will be *Thunderbolt*, 'cause you light up the stage."

Stinky, still unable to stand still, quickly embraced his new identity.

"That's me, boy! I'm Thunderbolt, TB on the stage!"

"TB onstage." The manager smiled. "This kid is a natural."

Wait, it got worse: Three groupies came out and held on to Marion's arms, and he didn't resist. He smiled as if he somehow deserved attention.

Then Marion said — rather gleefully, as he was obviously very pleased with his groupies — to the man in the sunglasses, "Hey, what do we call you?"

The man looked at him as if he'd just closed the deal. "Son, you can call me Moochie, 'cause I make the *moola!* Come on, we got a show to put on — thousands of fans screaming your name, bringing you flowers, and paying you at the same time."

Ryan was still stuck on how fast things were moving, but not unhappy with the progress. So, for clarification, he said, "I, me, Ryan, have a show to put on, with thousands of adoring fans?"

Moochie smiled at him and said, "No, *Rain Man* has a show to put on. Time we get to the studio — we only work with the best, and time is of the essence."

I could no longer contain my jealousy, so I said, "Hey, Moochie, can we come see this extravaganza?" I mean, seeing is believing.

"Of course, dear heart. You can come now and see the transformation."

I wanted to say, "No thanks, I have to throw up," as I watched Marion get fed grapes by three adoring fans, young girls who looked as if they should be in bed right now. Where were the parents in this place? I was no fan, no fan at all.

So, I said, rather reserved, "I like my entertainment on television."

"Well, everyone," Ryan said, "catch you at the show. I am off to be the star I was born to be."

What star were you born to be? You still wet your pants at night after a scary movie, I said in my head. What I actually said to him (rather sarcastically) was, "Bye, Rain Man — or will it be Pee-in-Your-Pants, especially in front of a crowd?"

"But they don't know that, so shut up," Ryan said. "Besides, this is my fantasy."

"No," Moochie said in a corrective tone. "This is no fantasy, this is all real." He held up a flyer announcing *The Rain Man and Thunderbolt in Concert Tomorrow Night.* "It's happening."

The boys and their adoring fans piled into Moochie's limo. As they drove off, the reality of being stuck in that place another night became an undeniable fact. And if that wasn't bad enough, standing on the side of the road like some sort of stray dog was a young boy around fourteen years old with a camera. At first, I thought he couldn't speak—he just stared at Sharie. Then he took her picture, and I lunged for the camera to take it from him. Where I come from, you can't just have strange people taking your pictures.

"What are you doing, crazy little girl?" the boy spoke. The sound of his voice stopped me from going after his camera and actually taking it.

"Look pervert, why don't you take your pictures elsewhere!"

"Why don't you calm down? I actually came over here to take pictures of Rain Man and Thunderbolt, but the limo just drove off, and then I saw her and I was like ..."

"What do you mean *her*?"

I looked back at Sharie, who was staring at the young boy. Now, I had seen Sharie have crushes on boys before, but this was something else, something deeper—she was speechless, and she can freaking *talk* here.

"Salle," said the boy. "I know you might not believe me, since we've just met. My name is Jeffery, my friends call me Jeff. I will never break or hurt Sharie at all. She's so beautiful, I bet a million stars are named after her."

Sharie smiled, and Jeffery snapped her pictures and then reached for her hand.

"She's too young for boyfriends," I protested. "If her grandmother was here, she would whup her butt. She's twelve."

"I'm thirteen!" Sharie immediately corrected.

"Well, she's going into middle school, and we can't date until we get out of middle school into high school. Sixteen, to be exact."

"I never liked that rule," Sharie said.

"Well, you never said anything. Besides, get your leg broke, and who gon' take care of that baby?"

"Get your leg broke, what do you mean?" Jeffery questioned.

"You know what I mean, Romeo. Get her leg broke, get herself in a helpless position with no support." I whispered to Sharie, "Like getting caught up, and you know what I mean."

"Don't worry, friend, I'm smarter than that!" Sharie said with an air of confidence—in fact, too much confidence.

The young boy put his camera back in his backpack, which I hadn't noticed at first, and then walked back over to Sharie and held both her hands. He asked her if she liked ice cream and she nodded yes, and they turned as if to walk away. I wanted to yell, "I hope you also like diarrhea, 'cause you're lactose intolerant, in case you forgot!" But I said nothing, slightly hoping she *would* get diarrhea. Would serve her right.

I hated this place. This couldn't be healthy, what was going on here. It was insane. My mama had told me, "Boys don't want nothing but a test dummy," when they are young like that, which was why she wouldn't allow me to date. She said dating was for mature adults. Now, had Sharie just matured? The same girl who snuck and ate her boogers on the down-low? The practical joker who put fart pillows on other kids' seats? A mature adult? Give me a break! We could talk about love, but we couldn't be in love, we were just kids. I had to say something!

So, while the two were standing there staring into each other's eyes, I said, "I hate to destroy the staring contest, but she's not allowed to do this. Her grandmother is crazy. She will fight a kid! And her mother wouldn't like this, let me tell you, she wouldn't like this one bit. Besides, we both made a pact not to date until we're juniors in high school. We're both only thirteen now, which means we have three more years to wait. We can't be here for three more years, so you ass out of luck, as my grandpa would say. So, young man, no-named boy, get to stepping."

"My name is Jeffery."

"My name is Sharie."

"And my name is ... Is Anyone Listening to Me?!"

But it appeared that somehow, Sharie had gotten lost in him. She was only aware of the boy whose name was Jeffery. What kind of a name was that, anyway?

Jeffery finally spoke. "I know you can't date and all. Really, I just want to listen to you. I have so many questions. Like, where did you come from? How did you get to know Rain Man and Thunderbolt? Hey, do you like to talk?"

"You have *no idea*," said Sharie.

"Maybe we can just go get ice cream and just talk? I mean, you talk and I listen," said Jeffery.

Sharie's eyes lit up, "Ice cream!"

I wasn't going to have any more of this, so I said, "Listen, Sharie, I have known you most of my life and you've known Jeffery — this strange kid with the camera — for what, five minutes? Are you going to listen to him or me, when I tell you — "

Sharie interrupted my speech; in fact, she ignored me completely, so I stopped talking.

"Who will drive us to go get the ice cream?" Sharie asked. And again, out of nowhere appeared a limo and driver.

"We are going to get ice cream," Sharie said to me with a dreamy smile. "Afterward, I will meet you at the concert."

Sharie was off, just like the other three — off to live a dream life. But not me. I was going to crack this case, even if I had to do it alone. "If only I had two other people just like me, I could do it quicker," I whispered to myself.

I sat on the diamond-covered sand, contemplating my problem and hammering out solutions in my head, when I noticed two girls around my same height and age sitting right next to me. I didn't want to speak, so I just ignored them and tried to wish them away in my mind, but they still sat there, like two toy soldiers waiting for me to direct them. I certainly didn't recall asking aloud for two new friends. Then, it hit me. I'd whispered it. *So, what we whisper will come true. I have got to remember that — no verbalized thoughts.*

So, there they were, my two new friends. I didn't like them, although this was what I needed most. It was my sincere hope that, whatever was happening in this place, my thoughts could not be understood, so, just for the heck of it, I decided to test it. In my mind, I commanded the two strangers to jump ten times. They didn't move. I felt reassured that, if nothing else, at least this place couldn't take my mind and my memory.

I was beginning to miss my regular life: My mother and her gentle (and sometimes stern) way of correcting me. My father. My uncle who irritated me, but in a weird way, protected me. I missed my older brother and his childish ways—OK, maybe I didn't miss him a whole lot, just a little. I even missed my grandfather asking one hundred questions when he knew I didn't want to talk.

I even missed my Auntie with her acting-grown self. She isn't the brightest bud on the tree, but she's my TT. Most people just call her Lil Mama 'cause she can act more grown than she actually is and take that TT role much too far; she is the princess of doing too much. I try not to be too hard on my TT. Her brothers are both at least twenty years older, and her mama didn't have any more kids, so we're all she's got.

Yeah, I missed my family and my life back in the hood. Or could it be that I simply felt safer in their presence? I looked at my watch and noticed that it was five o'clock. I didn't know if it was in the wee hours of the morning or the afternoon. I thought about my grandpa, the self-proclaimed war hero, who wakes us at 5 a.m. because he personally feels it's a sin to let the sun greet you in bed. If it is a sin to *not* let the sun greet you in bed, that is the only sin my grandpa won't commit. That man makes my brother and I get up most days at 5 a.m. to eat breakfast and get ready for school. On weekends, we still get up at 5 a.m. and have breakfast, but then go back to bed.

I wondered if my mother took that fish out like she said she might do, or if she cooked the spaghetti from scratch, or opened the Chef Boyardee from the can and simply added real tomato paste.

I really just wanted to be back to my normality, which was the West Side of Chicago. I wanted Ms. Nelson to catch us doing something bad and tell our parents. The only thing is, we would fix the problem before our parents would find out, so she would always sort of look like she was making up things on us (in which case, sometimes she would). However, that was life to me. The West Side of Chicago.

Before I allowed my emotions to cripple my self-determination and I totally succumbed to this bogus reality, I had to straighten myself out and *get some grit about myself* (as my grandfather liked to say when he thought we were lacking courage). The problem still at hand, though, was how do we get home? I watched the two girls sitting next to me who also appeared to be deep in thought and muttered to myself, "Back to reality—now how do I get us home?"

"Good question," one of the girls answered, and then it hit me they could talk.

My next and more logical question was, "Who are you two?"

They looked at each other and laughed as if enjoying a joke I was obviously not privileged to. Then the girl in a casual gray-and-green dress with a perfect fit stood up to speak. Even if I'd had the money, I don't think I could have picked a better fit. These girls had a nice sense of style, now that was a plus; I would have killed to have it myself—well not killed, but you get the point.

"You said you wished you had two more people like you, so here we are."

"So, are you *me*?" I asked, looking them over carefully for anything that resembled me and *definitely* finding some similarities.

"Don't be silly, Salle," said the girl in the gray-and-green dress. "I am Sallemae, and she's Sal, so don't start tripping. I mean, you ain't all that."

"I'm saying, calm down, girl," said Sal, as she quickly stood up, only to reveal that she and I also had the same sense of fashion. She was dressed in a cute red-and-white striped skirt

with a solid light blue T-shirt sprinkled nicely
with red dots. I thought her outfit was well put
together, and my mother told me you should
never hold back a compliment. So, I let her
know.

"That blue rocks with the red and white
skirt."

"I know, right?" Sal grinned, and she and I
said together, "Always put together the
unexpected." I looked at her and we laughed. If
only my mother *understood* this, we could
actually go shopping together, and I wouldn't
have to do it with my TT. Before I knew it, we
all were laughing together, and for a slight
moment, I had something to laugh about.

But the question—my quest, really—still
remained. How to get home? As much as I liked
these two girls who reminded me slightly of me,
they weren't my real friends and they wouldn't
be going home with me.

9

INSIDE LIKE MINDS

It seemed like hours but could have been mere minutes. In this place, there was very little need for sleep. I think I took maybe a five-minute nap and woke up refreshed to find that Sallemae and Sal were also awake and quite energetic.

We had a lot in common, which actually surprised me because I'm from a big city and both of these girls were from a small town. We acted alike, but certainly did not look alike. Sal had longer hair with red streaks, she was lighter in complexion, and she had small pimples on her forehead which she covered with makeup.

My hair was curlier by nature, even though in this imagination world my hair was down my back. Coarse hair was the best; my mother said that coarse hair was better because it could take more abuse. She should know—her hair had been cut, colored, permed, and Jheri-curled all in one year, and she still has hair. Although now she said she would be keeping it in braids so that it can grow out before she, of course, cuts it again.

Sallemae wore her hair off her face in a bun-like style. It appeared she needed glasses most of the time. She also frowned when she talked like she smelled something. I found myself checking to see if my breath stunk when she talked. It was irritating. And that bun, not really doing it for her. *Ughhh*, now I'm thinking about hair again. How I wish it wasn't such a big deal!

Anyway, Sallemae was a lot shorter, which was good because it helped me tell those two apart—they sounded exactly alike. They were the closest thing to common sense in the place. Most of the things I said, they absolutely agreed with. I wanted to trust them, but I really didn't yet. I wanted them to stay with me, though. No one wants to be alone.

I also decided to live a little. Now, it's not that I was off my rocker like my other four friends, but I had always wanted to live in a mansion and, since I was stuck here, I simply said "mansion" and it appeared, and there is where I resided. Pretty cool, right? I had a six-bedroom beachfront mansion in Learned Kansan.

It was strange, though. It was almost as if I were living on a different beach in a different place. Learned Kansan felt eerie to me. It's like when you look in a magazine and you can imagine the place, but it's not like really being there. This place felt like people tried so hard to bring to life what this place felt like, but they got a few things wrong. The only thing I am absolutely sure about Learned Kansan is that animals, at some point, were being slaughtered. That smell was unmistakable. When I traveled south and visited my uncle's farm, there was the same smell.

It was something about the smell of this beach that was different. The other beach I'd visited in Chicago smelled like Febreze or detergent. This beach smelled like dying fish, crabs, or seawater. This beach where my mansion was located had just plain white sand, no glistering diamonds.

I liked my mansion. It was just the right size, and it was already decorated to my liking with very little furniture. One room simply had a couch, a throw rug, and a picture of the ocean. It was nice. Sallemae and Sal enjoyed this as well, especially when we created sleds out of cardboard boxes and went down the banisters. We also took pleasure in having a maid do things for us — you know, stuff I hated doing at home, like making my bed and hanging up clothes.

It tickled me how clean my room was in this place. My mother said being rich isn't all it's cracked up to be; well, Mother, I can honestly say that can only be said if you've never lived it. In fact, it is *all it's cracked up to be,* if not more. I ordered food. I had friends who always agreed with me and admired me at the same time. I had a closet full of cool clothes I knew I wouldn't ever wear—but they provided options, and nothing is better than options.

I had a movie theater right in my mansion. Sal and Sallemae took pleasure in watching movies and having me change the ending. It was *sooo* much fun, I almost forgot I wanted to leave. I even so much as said, "I forgot I wanted to leave," and if it had not been for Sallemae's casual comment, "Then just stay, girl," I would have lost sight of the mission and the fact that it was getting close to the time for the concert.

They had heard of the new rap sensations, Rain Man and Thunderbolt. They loved hearing me talk about how I'd met Rain Man and Thunderbolt and were surprised that Thunderbolt was called Stinky in Chicago, and that Rain Man was really Ryan, a non-rappin' juvenile delinquent—well, he had never gone to jail, but he was at best a future juvenile delinquent (him and Stinky both).

It wasn't until my new purple-and-white outfit arrived that I realized that I had, in fact, done most of the talking, and that these two snappy, nappy, mess-of-a-teens were actually good listeners. However, I needed them to stop listening and start talking so that I could learn how to get back home. As we sat and painted our toes, it was time for me to play twenty-one questions, and my ears were ready to listen.

"So, tell me, Sal and Sallemae, are you related? You sort of look alike."

They looked at each other, I guess to see who would be the one to answer, and just as I had expected, it was Sallemae. She seemed to really like to be first in things.

She cleared her throat and said, rather uncomfortably, "Actually, we are sisters. In fact, and this is weird, we were born on the same day, but we are not twins. I was born a year before Sal, on April tenth."

"Yep, April tenth," Sal chimed in as if she were Sallemae's personal "Amen" section.

Another something we had in common—birthdays—for my birthday was also April tenth, but for some reason, I wasn't going to confirm this with them. Nope, I wasn't going to do that at all.

Instead, I asked, "Where are you from originally, or have you always lived here?"

After some laughter and another awkward pause, Sallemae again spoke first. "Well, actually we are from New York. My clock always stays on New York time. But originally, I mean. We're here now, and kinda sorta from ... this place. We've lived here, like, forever."

"What place?" I asked.

"This place, right here," she answered, and I could see the wheels turning, as if she was fishing for the name of this place. I found it hard not to supply her with the name, but I wasn't going to let her off the hook that easily, so I asked again.

"What place?"

This time, Sal jumped in and bailed her out and said, "Learned Kansan. This is home to us all. People don't just appear here, silly."

"Well, I did," I reminded her, and again, she was a little taken aback. I wondered what Sal was referring to, so I reiterated, "What do you mean things don't just appear? Of course they do. I mean, *you speak it, you get it* sort of things. That's the joy of living in Learned Kansan, better known as Middle Heaven."

The girls looked at each other, for they knew in all their getting they had let me get something. So, I asked, "Tell me, sisters, at some point in this fantasy world things stop being as you hope them to be. This is all going to end, and when it ends—what will life be like then?"

"Things will always be magical in this place, that's the fun of it all," Sal said, as if she had just discovered this truth herself.

Just to test this theory, I asked Sal and Sallemae how they wanted to arrive in style for the big concert, then I stopped them from telling me. I simply told them to surprise me.

Now the girls had to come up with a way for us to get to the concert without me saying it first. *Yeah, Learned Kansan, I am learning all I need to know about you.* At first I was angry at my real-world friends and their blissful ignorance. We were street kids and knew a thing or two about games, and it surprised me that they didn't see the game in all this.

What happened to the popular phrase, "If it looks too good to be true, chances are it is"? Now, I was not angry at my friends. I felt sorry for them. Tonight, after the concert, I would have a heart-to-heart with them. Maybe it would be me who would need to change.

Which was why I found myself stuck between emotions. I wanted them to experience all the joy this place would give them, but I desperately needed them to remember what we'd left behind and what could be lost. Also, I knew a little something else they didn't know — that all of this would end. The girls so much as told me that. Although I am not so sure how they got here from New York, I am sure that there are things I can do that they cannot do, which leads me to infer that things will definitely end.

The question is, when? When does all this favor end? On that thought, I asked my newfound pretend friends again, "So, tell me how we'll be getting to the concert? Your choice. . . and please use your imaginations."

10

ROMANCE IN THE AIR, SHARIE

Jeffery and Sharie spent hours exploring mountains throughout the world. They landed on Mount Elbert, in Colorado—the highest summit of the Rocky Mountains of North America and the highest point in the State of Colorado. Then they spent what appeared to be hours at the Mississippi River, listening to the *whoosh* and *slush* sounds, like what she imagined snow under her feet would sound like. When the waters were silent, it sounded like wind, teasing the atmosphere with a very soft cry, or like drizzling rain softly baptizing dry skin, faint but ever-present.

After Jeffery and Sharie took in a meal, they went back to climbing. Sharie had always longed to visit such places while in Chicago, and had even told her grandmother she wanted to learn to climb, just to be told, "Black people don't climb," which she had since learned was not true. Anyway, she'd never really understood why she needed a reason to want to do the things she wanted to do. Like, what the heck did race have to do with it anyway? Why did she need a reason to like climbing or drawing, or why did she need a reason for wanting to travel? She just wanted to do it like she wanted to dance — it looked fun.

For the first time in her life, she finally had someone with whom she could share those things. As light and fun as those moments felt to her, she also had to admit something else: she was able to hear. And she was able to share the fact that now, she hears fear, and that's something she'd never heard before. Fear to her felt like dreadful footsteps approaching her, and when it got close enough to touch her, it passed by her.

She realized she was afraid of lots of things and wondered how the hearing world learned not to be afraid of all the things. She began to realize it was the hearing that caused the heart to soar or sink; it was the hearing that turned your emotional world out upside-down, leaving you wishing you had never known. So, for moments she blocked out sound and went back into her deep world of not knowing — not knowing that all that was right about this world meant that there must be an equally dark side.

Now with sound, she had to count on what Jeffery told her: "Don't jump," "Don't touch," "Be still," "A mountain lion might be near." And so, she found herself afraid often, but mostly afraid of what she knew must be true. She was able to push the fear to dark places.

Sharie really liked Jeffery because he was a good listener, and all her life she had wanted someone to listen to her, so she talked and talked and even talked some more, waiting for a slight sign that maybe Jeffery was tired of listening. But he never gave one—he never yawned, rolled his eyes, or looked away, but rather sat in front of her, or at her side, and just listened. He listened so well she never had to ask, "Are you listening?" even after what appeared to be hours.

"God is about to close his curtain," Sharie said.

"What does that mean?" Jeffery giggled.

"That means God is about to blanket the sky with darkness. Close his curtains. Bedtime."

Jeffery smiled, and she could see that she had amused him.

"My grandmother used to say that a lot," Sharie said.

"She must have had some personality."

"She has *some personality alright*. She's still alive. She's like my rock, but she can be a little mean, and straightforward, judgmental, overbearing—you get the point."

"Sure do!"

They smiled at each other. That night, they had shared many things, but that would be all; unlike what Salle might think, she was a smart girl. Actually, Salle may never know how much Sharie really admired Salle's holy boldness, but Salle could be a little overbearing herself. Sharie liked Jeffery, but she wasn't going to let him take her gold. Another phrase her grandmother always said, "Don't let no boy take your gold." She giggled.

"Will you tell me more about your grandmother and school soon?" Jeffery said.

"I want a small cabin to sleep in for the night ... with twin beds," said Sharie.

He smiled, and, of course, he got the point. No one was going to take her gold this night or any night *soon*. However, she wanted to be able to look at him. He was beautiful to her. His smiling eyes and gentle giggle—just beautiful— and he may know this or not, but tonight she would pray that one day she would meet him again in her world.

As she lay beside him before sleep had subdued her, she decided that she would end the night listening for a while.

"What is it really, Jeffery?"

"What is what?"

"Is this a dream, or what?"

"I'm very real, Sharie, and you are very beautiful."

She couldn't bear to say another word that night. In fact, she didn't want to hear another thing that night. If all she had were those words, she could feed on them for days, and she wouldn't ever die of hunger. Maybe her friend would one day understand, and maybe she would herself understand, but those words massaged her heart in ways she hoped the world would experience, and if this was love, it was a beautiful thing. It was the love that kept the fear at bay.

The next day, they awoke to the sun beaming from a mountaintop. She was so enchanted with the surroundings, she forgot she could speak. Jeffery was up and dressed; he had on a bright green turtleneck sweater and blue jeans. Hidden behind his back was a brown paper bag. Before she could say a word, he was guiding her to a chair. Food was cooking in the kitchen, but she didn't bother to ask who was doing the cooking. He waited until she was seated and settled, then brought out the brown bag. He handed it to her.

"What's this?" she asked.

"Just open it."

"A journal? You brought me a journal."

"Just for you, and no matter what happens, make sure you take it with you. My gift."

"Why a journal?"

"You tell really good stories. I thought you might like to one day write it all out. After we eat, tell me about your school days. Sounds like fun."

"Well, I don't know that much about *fun*— just before we came to this wonderful place, we were on our way to being in detention for the whole summer."

"Why?" Jeffery asked with genuine interest.

Sharie went on to tell him about the science lab disaster, and how it really wasn't her fault, but boy, wasn't it fun! She explained their challenge, which was simply to do ten good things before the summer was over, and how this was almost impossible because she was sure they wouldn't find ten good things to do, and even if they wanted to do the ten good things, one of them would for sure mess up. Then she noticed that look in his eyes again—a look that said, "I got a secret, and I really want to tell you, but I can't."

Or was he saying this in whisper form? With her ability to hear sound, her judgment was a bit off. She began to miss again the times when her friends didn't have to tell her when they were angry. She usually felt it. She just never knew how to fix things, which was why she got into trouble so much.

She was going for it—maybe he really wanted to be kissed? So, with full, passionate intention, she went in with the lips, puckered up and out. All he had to do was lean toward her with his lips for the landing. Clearly, she had made the first move. She wouldn't let him take her gold, but her lips he could have. He came in and they gently kissed, right on the lips. Time ticked by, grandma-style—what seemed like hours had been mere seconds. They kissed, he had kissed her, and that was all she wanted.

"I—Thank you?" he said, unsure of his response.

She didn't know what to say, but "You're welcome" just weren't the words her heart wanted to speak, so her silence spoke as she held on tightly to her journal. He didn't know that writing was one of the few subjects she hated in school. But today, everything would change. Everything had changed.

The next few hours flew by quickly. Sharie was tired of talking and wanted to climb more, and not those small mountains either. So, she spoke it: "Let's climb that mountain," and "Give me what I need."

"So, you ready to climb?" Jeffery said. "That's what I'm good at."

"Great, let's go again."

They walked to the door and found backpacks waiting.

"Mountaineering involves lots of gear," Jeffery said confidently.

"I see. This is going to be fun," Sharie said.

"Wait a minute, young lady. Mountaineering requires more than athleticism. It takes patience and precision."

For the first time, Sharie knew they had crossed a line into a field Jeffery knew lots about. He bundled her up with a backpack and they went outside. Sharie couldn't wait to explore what was inside the pack. She opened it and found an ice axe, food packages, a flashlight, two water bottles … "We're really hooked up for this climb," she said to herself.

When they got outside, Sharie noticed a Labrador retriever—a friendly dog who came right up and licked her hands. Sharie patted her side pocket and found dog treats. She gave him one.

"Great," said Jeffery, "it's always good to travel with an animal." He was surprised to see the dog, but he welcomed the friendly new pet.

"We got four hours," said Sharie, ready to hit the road — or rocks, so to speak.

Jeffery grabbed her by the hand, and they headed off in the direction of the mountain; Sharie was already breathless in anticipation. For a brief second, she thought about Salle and what she might be doing or thinking. Sharie wondered if Salle wished for friends, or even if she still considered them her friends. Rather than thinking about it quietly, Sharie decided she would rather talk about it, so as they climbed, Jeffery got to hear all about Salle.

Jeffery was quiet for much of the climb. He explained at one point that people never have to look for reasons to be good, good usually presents itself to you. Sharie thought to herself, *That's something I should remember when I get back home ...*

Back home lingered in her mind like a diet coke aftertaste. *Home* — it was starting to feel obsolete. She didn't let it worry her much, though. Her goal right now was to feel the accomplishment of the climb.

They climbed for three hours, and boy was Sharie tired. The dog they'd named Buck carried their backpacks. Sharie got tired; climbing was not what she expected, but she still enjoyed it. She realized that Jeffery had been trying to warn her about not being in shape to really climb. After they climbed four thousand feet, they would have to return back down the same distance.

Jeffery said that was good, and maybe it was, but Sharie wasn't about to climb down; climbing the four thousand feet took all of four hours. No way was she climbing back down. That would have to be her next adventure! She simply spoke, "Back in the cabin," and there they were.

Sharie loved being able to do that! *I need Middle Heaven at home with me sometimes. Who wouldn't like living life a little in Middle Heaven?*

Sharie took her tired body and soaked it for all of thirty minutes. She was tired, but this concert she had to go to. She got dressed in a beautiful gray-and-black pantsuit and she let her hair just hang down her shoulders. This made her feel grown, because she was a kissed woman now. She would forever remember that experience, whether she was in Middle Heaven or at home.

She found Jeffery sitting deep in thought. She wasn't able to really pin his emotions. He looked happy sometimes and worried other times. She caught the look of sympathy in his eyes, and this sickened her. She hated people feeling sorry for her. But then she reasoned that maybe he was just tired. She knew this concert would cheer him up—for although he wore a smile on his face, there was something else there.

"I think it's time to go to the concert."

"Cool!" Jeffery responded. "How do you want to go? We can fly, take a plane, or ride a train. What's your pleasure, Sharie?"

"The limo will get us there, right?"

He smiled at her and reached for her hands, but little did he know he had her heart as well. "Let's go!" he said confidently.

Sharie didn't get the sense anymore that he wanted to tell her something, and in a heartbeat they were back in the limo, heading to the concert to see Stinky and Ryan perform. It wasn't as though she was looking forward to it. They were silly little boys and the concert would be silly too, of course. But she would laugh and pretend to like it. What she couldn't wait to do was wake up in this place again and go to Disney World with Jeffery. She hoped he wanted to go with her.

Disney World, now that was living! After Disney World, that may just be it for her, for she was slowly missing Grandma and all the things that came with being home. She had to admit it: the more she enjoyed this place, the more distant those thoughts became. It was like sometimes her home felt like the fantasy and this place felt more like home.

She was sure it was Jeffery that was making the difference. She imagined what her family might be doing right about now. She was sure her mother had stopped by for a meal or two, and money. Grandma probably *checked* her mother, or, as she would say, "Wrecked her world with a dose of truth and let her know who's really in control."

Her mother would have to bow down, for she knew deep down inside it was Grandma who got things done around the house. After that, Grandma would whip up something spectacular for dinner and all would be forgiven. Granny often wouldn't eat, but it was pure satisfaction she got from watching her daughter eat.

When the lights were low and time was plentiful and Granny had time to practice her sign language, she would often sign that she wished she had been there more for Sharie's mother, but that when Sharie grew up, she would have no excuse. Some days, Sharie didn't see her mother at all, but her mother told her not to worry. If for some reason she didn't stop by, don't worry — somehow or someway she would always be there, either on this earth or in the sky. She's OK.

When Sharie thought about it, she missed them, but she didn't want to miss them too badly, because she was having too much fun. Her life in Chicago could wait.

11

ROCKING IT

We had slid down banisters and eaten soul food, with peach cobbler for dessert. Sal and Sallemae even let me pick out their outfits. I put them both in purple. I don't know, I just figured I was the one speaking things to life, and they certainly wouldn't out-dress me on this historic night, so I put them both in purple jumpsuits. Sallemae didn't like it, but I didn't care; she could just speak herself into something different if she liked.

The purple twins — as I called them — were all ready to go. We stood around for minutes just looking and giggling at each other until it began to irritate me. So, I asked again, "How are we getting there?"

"There — where?" asked Sal.

I had concluded that Sal wasn't the brightest of the two, so either she wanted to look stupid or she was just being plain stupid. Either way, I was on to her.

"Sal, to go where we're dressed up to go."

"Oh," interjected Sallemae, "We said it's all up to you, dear."

OK, wait a minute. These two mini-mes thought they could play me? I'd had to humor them for hours, telling them all about my life. I'd even pretended to like them and invited them to stay in my mansion. Now they were tryin' to play me … *me*!

"Who y'all think you playing?" I demanded furiously.

"Who you think *you* playing?" Sallemae struck back just as furiously.

"Well, I tell you what, you better speak up a ride or come clean, or we miss the concert."

I sat on the steps of my beautiful mansion, ready to do the next best thing, which was to kick out these smart-mouthed know-it-alls who don't know anything. They had swindled my good nature, manipulated my emotions, caused me to create problems for them to solve, and now it was over.

Speak or forever hold your peace, I thought, but I wasn't budging. They looked at each other as if they had some sort of private, silent communication with each other, then looked back at me with pity, but I wasn't moving. They must have forgotten I was a bit of a hard nut to crack. Finally, Sallemae sat next to me and said, somewhat consolingly, "Well it does make Learned Kansan less appealing, but at some point, you do sort of lose the power to speak things right up."

At this point, Sal jumped right in. "This does not lessen the fun of the place. I mean, it's still gon' rock. We been here for like, forever, and do you see us getting tired?"

I gave her the only answer I knew was truthful, "Yes, I see you getting tired. So, how long?"

"Now here's the thing—" Sal started to say before Sallemae cut her off.

"Look, it's different for most people. We don't know. I guess it's when you've been every place you want to go, seen everything you want to see, done all you want to do, and you say, 'No more,' then it's over."

She was lying. Of course, she didn't sound like a liar, but she was lying, because I caught the spark in Sal's eyes when the lie came out of Sallemae's mouth; you could tell she was both shocked and pleased to hear this rationalization. But I wasn't having it. What I needed was for them to turn against each other, so I said, "I'm not buying it."

"And why not?" asked Sallemae.

"Because when you made that statement, I looked at Sal and she was like, shocked—like really surprised that you brought it like that."

"That's a lie!" said Sal.

"It's not a lie. Go ahead and admit it. You had your own story, but Sallemae, like the controlling monster she is, couldn't trust your story, so she created her own. Who knows, your story could have been better."

"Well, yeah, it could have but—" started Sal.

"Shut up, stupid!" interrupted Sallemae. "Maybe you're just mad that I got it right."

OK, now this was what I wanted—a fight. When people are angry, they have little self-control. I could see all Sal heard was "*stupid.*" So, in the moment, and knowing this love affair could end, I said, "Who she calling stupid? I know she ain't talking to *me.*"

"Of course not," Sallemae said.

"I know you ain't talking to *me,*" said Sal, "'cause baby, I ain't never stupid. You the stupid one!"

"No baby, you the stupid one! But it's cool, only five more days with you."

"Five more days with you!"

"Wait a minute, let's not get all dramatic and mess up our hair," I said. "We do have a show to go to. So, let the limo come get us." Just as before, a white limo appeared and we all jumped in.

The girls had told me a whole lot, and I didn't want them gone just yet. I had learned that Learned Kansan wasn't always going to be so much fun, and, more than likely, it would end in five days. So, I had four more days to get my friends out of this place.

The ride in the limo was cold. They were mad at me and each other. As for me, I was having fun, because that was what they wanted me to do in Learned Kansan. *But next time, before this place starts sending me friends, it had better check them out better is all I'm saying.*

12

THE SHOW

When we made it to the concert, we were quickly ushered behind the stage through a back door. I didn't even have to ask where to go because my girls, Sal and Sallemae, led the way. There were a lot of people in the backstage area—a lady with an earpiece checking the clothes, a man carrying coffee, several men pulling in amps and checking lights. There were big pictures of Stinky and Ryan on a poster.

I looked behind the heavy black curtains and saw several thousand people, young girls and boys, shouting and holding pictures of Rain Man and Thunderbolt. *Man, they really know how to dream for real*, I thought. But oh, this was not just a dream; this was them in the future. Well, it looked good, but I had to make sure they realized that this little something special they had dreamed up was going to end ... soon.

When I entered the larger back room, I saw Ryan and Stinky for the first time. Ryan's red hair was slicked back and he was wearing all black. He had a gold chain the size of Learned Kansan around his neck and one earring. I knew one thing: he'd better get that out of his ear before he got home.

Stinky was dressed in all gold. He also had a long gold chain and was wearing dark shades. Someone had waved his hair and added a little gold dust on the top of his head to give it a matching look with his clothes. They looked all grown up and clownish. Rappers, what a trip.

As soon as Stinky laid eyes on me, he burst out, "Look, Salle, we big rap stars now; all those people out there are waiting to see us! Ryan said you wouldn't come to the concert, but I told him you would come."

Stinky gave me a hug. Ryan came over and gave me a peck on the cheek. Ryan and I really don't like being mad at each other; I could tell he wanted me to see him as a rapper. I didn't, but for today I would pretend as if I did. If I knew that it would last longer, I would be happier. But I was afraid he might not be able to handle the rejection, so I knew I had to say something—I just didn't know when.

Marion tore himself away from his three teenage companions and joined our circle. I wondered if the time was now, for it was just the four of us, but as soon as I thought the timing could have been right, one of the girls came over and whispered to Marion.

"Hey, Marion, why don't you send her away?"

The nerve of her to send *me* away. "This is a five-year friendship!" I wanted to say. "How long have you known him? Hours, I'm guessing." I would've swung on that chick had we been in Chicago, but it's cool; I knew Marion didn't roll like that.

There was something he wanted to tell me, so he told her to wait over by the door for him. She walked over — or rather, strode over, as if she was a runway model. However, I had to tell him, "I don't understand why that little fast-tail girl feels the need to walk that way. Who's she trying to impress?"

"She kissed me," said Marion, with an uneasiness that was almost embarrassing.

This excited Ryan and Stinky and they gave each other high fives. I just stared at Marion. Then Ryan whispered, "Think she'll go all the way?"

"No, no," answered Marion. "She said she's got to get to know me first."

OK, that was it! It was time. Before anyone "got to know" each other, I was going to tell them all the things I had learned. But then Sharie rushed in. She ran to the inner circle and hugged everyone—but of course, she was a hugger.

"Where have you been, Sharie?"

"Almost everywhere! I had lunch on the mountaintop, four thousand feet up! Jeffery is wonderful! You got to get to know him, Salle. He listens to me; I mean *really* listens to me!"

"Well, that's going to end in four days," I muttered under my breath.

"What?" Sharie asked with a very clueless tone.

I was about to say it, to just tell them everything while we were by ourselves, but before I could get a word out, Gill showed up with flowers for the boys. Their manager, Moochie, followed. After giving each of us a very superficial kiss, he pulled Stinky and Ryan away from the group and led them backstage.

"I guess it's showtime for them," Sharie said with a cynical undertone.

"Yeah. Ladies?" Marion clapped his hands and the girls were at his side. Then they went out together.

I looked at Sharie, wanting to tell her she looked beautiful. I always thought she would look good in a pin-up. Some male servants came over, took her hands, and then walked her away from me. Usually, she would ask me how she looked and if what she had on matched. I guess she really didn't need me anymore. She was learning to trust her own judgment. Sal came over, interrupting my pity party.

"What's wrong, girlfriend?" Sal asked.

"Nothing," I answered, then added, "It's just that, when we're home, Sharie usually asks me how she looks. I guess she doesn't need my opinion now."

"Well, she should have asked your opinion before she half-pinned up her hair like that. I mean, really, child," Sal responded.

"I like the pin-up," I said sincerely.

"Me too. I just thought it could have been a little neater," Sal said.

"But she looked better with a pin-up," added Sallemae, "that's all we're trying to say."

No, that's not what she was trying to say at all, but it was cool. I knew what *I* had to say, as soon as the concert ended. I walked to the back of the stage and took my seat front and center.

My two newly found fake best friends sat next to me and the show began with a loud, boastful announcement of the two famous artists, lights flashing at an incredibly fast rate. Had I been epileptic, I probably would have fainted; ambulance sounds and alarms were going off all over the place while smoke was coming up from the front of the stage. My first thought was *I hope Stinky didn't start a fire*, and this would have been a practical theory until the two clowns emerged from the sky, hanging from almost-invisible ropes. They landed front and center, legs apart, hands folded in front of them as if they were top-rate bodyguards — but obviously they had been trained and practiced this a lot.

I would have bought it until they opened their mouths. One could only imagine what we were in store for now. That *show*.

13

THAT SHOW, THAT SHOW, THAT SHOW, THAT *SHOW*

I am just a thirteen-year-old, and I can be jealous at times, I will admit. But never in a million years would I be jealous of this show. They sang the same song in five different ways for one-and-a-half hours.

First, it was "Spank That Butt," then "Move That Butt," then "Groove That Butt," and since that wasn't enough, they led us into "You Mad 'Cause You Ain't Got a Butt." Lastly, for the grand finale, we got "Don't Be Mad at My Butt." And for every single song, Ryan had only one sentence, and Stinky just repeated that one sentence.

I honestly wanted to kill those two. We could have been back home in bed! I looked from time to time to see if Marion and Sharie were enjoying this, but they were too into their individual arm candy to worry about the tragedy that was happening on the stage. The audience, all young girls, was yelling, screaming, and fainting all over the place. Every time they started a new song, you'd see kids passing out.

Was this the show these boys wanted? The obnoxious talent displayed on stage was giving me the strength to speak my mind. Sallemae and Sal, as phony as those two girls were, couldn't even fake they liked the show, so they sat watching me as I watched the show. They witnessed my growing anger as the show progressed. I went from *I can't take this* with head bowed to *You can't be for real*, head bowed, eyes closed.

Afterward, everyone was moving toward backstage. I rushed ahead and cleared out the side dressing room. Sal and Sallemae wanted to be with me 'cause they had some choice words about the concert, but I sent them away. If someone had to hurt my friends' feelings, it would be me. I signaled for Sharie to come in. She tried to bring in her boy-toy, *Jeffery*, but I told him this conference was private. Marion, as if he knew what was going to happen, walked right in, alone.

Around forty minutes later, the superstars finally walked in. So, there they all were, Sharie,

Marion, Ryan, and Stinky, staring at me as if I was the dessert and they were hungry. I didn't feel any support in the room, but we were alone, and I could say what I needed to say and then we could leave. So, I gave it to them straight.

"What was *that*?" I asked. I really didn't want an answer, but I got one anyway.

"The show? It was incredible, unbelievable!" said Marion.

"I thought it was cool myself," agreed Sharie.

"Are you crazy?" I asked in disbelief. "It was horrible! Every song they sang had one word in common — 'butt' — and there was only one phrase per song."

"So, what's wrong with that?" yelled Stinky.

"What's right with it?" I demanded. "And what's with these people fainting all over the place? That was so phony! This place is all just one big mess."

"You should have worn green, not purple," Ryan said.

"Oh, yeah? Well, you shouldn't ever slick your hair back like that again."

I had to take a deep breath. I was getting too defensive and I really needed them to listen to me. "Anyway, what I really want to say is that we've got to get out of this place. I am not sure, but I think we have to leave within five days, or else—"

"We've got a tour and it don't end till Saturday," said Stinky.

"But we have to leave within five days. Don't you see? If we want to leave, it has to be before Saturday or—or things could go bad."

"What do you mean, 'bad'?" asked Sharie.

I wasn't altogether sure what I meant, but I had a feeling, and so I went for my theory.

"We could get stuck in this place, like, for life, and never see our parents again," I whispered.

They all looked at me in silence, and for the first time in twenty-four hours, I thought I was getting through to them. Ryan picked up his leather jacket and said, rather calmly, "For the first time, this is not about you, Salle. You've always been the smart one. You play the violin. You get the highest scores on the quizzes and tests. It's the Salle show. But here in Learned Kansan, it's *our show*, and you can't handle that, can you, Salle?"

"What I can't handle is you having only half a brain," I said. But I wished I hadn't. He was wrong, but that statement made him sound so right, and they were leaving, my last hope. They were all walking away from me in silence, which meant we couldn't even fight it out. I grabbed Marion by the arm.

"Marion, why is it you have to wait until five days? It's just a kiss or whatever, right? I know I can be a little controlling, and a know-it-all at times, but you've got to believe me. Did you really see talent on that stage? They said the same thing literally for an hour and a half."

"MC Hammer had the top song in America and all he said was "Can't touch this," Marion said.

He walked away, and with him went my only hope. Marion had always been the one person I could count on for a last-minute revelation. Sharie and I were always on the same page, but this Jeff guy had got her speaking a different language, just saying. How was I to convince this nutty crew of friends that we had to get back home?

As they walked out, in walked Sal and Sallemae.

"So," said Sal, "how did things go?"

"It was horrible!" I said. "I tried to tell them we should leave, but they wouldn't budge. They're so hard-headed."

"Especially if they think they're gonna make it on *that* talent. Really, it was the same dumb song, sung over and over," said Sallemae.

147

"That's what I'm saying. You heard that, right?"

"It was *horrible*. Who didn't hear it? So, you're saying they wanna stay anyway?" Sal asked, a little too happily.

"Well, I'm not going to say they want to stay, but they really do want to finish the concert. Dumb kids."

"Exactly. So we might as well go home and pop some popcorn. I have a bit of a headache after all that noise," Sallemae said.

"Yeah," I said, "let's go home and make popcorn, the one thing I can always eat. You remembered."

"Of course. We're your friends for real, miss lady," Sal said soothingly.

I was hurting and I really wanted to leave. That's when it hit me, and I said it aloud: "Dumb MC Hammer."

"Hate that song, 'Can't Touch This,'" said Sal.

"Me too," agreed Sallemae.

I stayed quiet about "Can't Touch This," 'cause that had been my and Ryan's favorite song. Then I realized that the beat they used for all the songs they sang that night was the same as "Can't Touch This." That explained the baggy gold pants Stinky had on today.

Well, well, well … so there was no originality in this place after all. It was all just a mirror or reflection of what you wanted in life. I was convinced that none of it was real; but if any of it was real, it was only temporary. It couldn't last.

"Take me home," I said. "I got work to do." The girls touched my arm and we were all on the steps of the beach mansion. I looked around the beach and felt like this place was out-of-place—who puts a mansion on a beach? But I had clothes in the closet I still wanted to check out, so I let the place remain for the time being.

14

GILL WHO?

When I was at home and things got really heavy on my mind, I would crawl underneath my bed and hide from the world, my thoughts, judgment, and, of course, consequences. When I was around six years old, I would go to my secret hiding place; my mother would come into my room and sit on my bed and pretend like she didn't know I was there and sort of explain to me the things she hoped I would do.

Like the time I accidentally bent my father's golf club. I didn't mean to do it, I simply needed something bigger to swat at the bees with, and I accidentally hit the club too hard against the porch steps. I knew my father was going to be mad at me because it was his lucky club. So, I hid away from everything that reminded me of my doom.

My mother calmly sat on my bed, wondering aloud where I was at. Then she explained that

151

when you do something wrong, the best thing you can do is simply fess up and tell the truth. She reminded me that my father loved me and although he would be mad at me, and I might have to stay in the house for a couple of days, he would eventually get over it, get another lucky club, and life would go on. It was the comfort of her voice that gave me the courage to face my fears. Later that day, I confessed to my dad, and because I told the truth, he only took away my television privileges for the weekend.

The point of this story is that there was this place I could go to get away from the world, where only truth could find me. In Learned Kansan, all I had were two talking sisters who asked way too many questions. I must admit, they were funny. Their take on Ryan and Stinky's performance was hilarious. I was laughing and crying at the same time. They had their dance down pat.

They wondered (as I did) how Ryan could turn around so much and not get dizzy. The only thing he'd really learned from this place was how to spin around like MC Hammer. Ryan the Rain Man, coolest rapper in No Man's Land. Even at the thought of this, I giggled to myself, just to find the girls were giggling with me. Maybe they thought I found something that they did or said funny, when actually, for the last however many minutes, I had been only irritated by them.

I needed just a little more information, and it was clear that these girls were on a need-to-know sort of deal with me. However, who would know it all? Who was the first person we'd met when we'd landed here? Gill. I needed to know more about Gill.

So, I said, "Take me to Gill's house."

You would have thought I'd just asked those girls to commit murder. They looked at each other before, of course, Sallemae answered.

"Girl, that's crazy. Why would anyone want to go to Gill's house?"

"I'm not anyone, I am Salle with an E, and I want to go to his house. He seems like an interesting man."

"That's crazy," said Sal. "He's not interesting at all. In fact, he is rather boring."

"You guys think he's boring?"

They each looked at each other, as if to get approval, before agreeing that "Gill is boring."

"Well," I said rather matter-of-factly, "the only person you guys talked to tonight was Gill. In fact, I caught you guys whispering in the corner to him. So, tell me about him."

"There's nothing to tell. He's boring, but a looker," said Sallemae.

"So, you have a crush on him," I said.

"No!" she shouted, as if that was forbidden.

"I want to go. I think I might like getting to know the dude. I'm told when people get to know me, they like me."

"I think he will like you less," said Sal.

The thing about Sal is that sometimes the truth escapes—that or she thinks less and doesn't know how to guard her tongue. I disliked them both; their flattery of me was superficial. In fact, they were a couple of supercilious misfits. They thought they understood who I was because they agreed with me on almost everything.

One thing they should have gathered from me is that I tend to aim at what I want, and I wanted to know more about Gill, and since it was clear we weren't going to agree, I grabbed the girls by the hands as I shouted, "Take us inside Gill's house."

We landed inside a large room with dim yellow lights. We had shrunk to the size of about two feet, and I was about to yell, but Sallemae held my mouth tight with her hands. Then she whispered with tears in her eyes, "Don't talk. Everything in here is living, and everything can communicate."

We ran behind a table that was made up of what appeared to be a thousand roaches—they were big with large, black eyes on the tops of their heads, and long antennas coming out the fronts of their heads that looked like stick pens. If I was at home, I would step on them and enjoy the crunchy sound they made under my shoe as the gooey white stuff stuck to the floor.

The small, round couch was made of locusts. Every now and again, the locusts made a floral smell, like dying flowers coming out right at us, hitting us in the face. I wanted to cough, but Sallemae held my mouth again. I noticed that the locusts shifted, moving just a little, making the couch look as if it was vibrating. It was oddly beautiful, and yet so weird. You had to question why a man like Gill would want to live in a house full of locusts.

The eyes of the locusts were open, but they didn't move, and I could only assume they must have been asleep. I'd never realized until now how much locusts and grasshoppers looked alike. Now we were small and they were big, and I got a chance to see how we must feel to something like a roach.

The ceiling was made up of bubble-eyed frogs. Their slimy skins were glittering and excreting slimy white stuff. They opened their eyes, and we closed our eyes, hoping they wouldn't jump on us. One big green frog with brown spots looked as if it was going to jump right at us, so we covered our heads. Instead, it jumped right past us, ate one fly that fell to the floor, jumped right back to its place, and went back to sleep. That was scary — a close call.

In the center of this room hung a dimly lit chandelier made of flies. That explained the slight buzzing sound I heard and the occasional frog food falling from the sky.

There were a few other rooms in this house, but we were obviously in the main room. Sal was now crying silent tears, but I couldn't move. I gave her my mother's cut-that-out look, but apparently, she couldn't help it. One of her tears dropped to the floor, and that's when I saw it.

Gill's floor was made of what appeared to be thousands of rectangular glass cases, and inside the cases were people. I stopped to wonder — this could not be explained. Why would Gill want glass cases full of people seemingly stuck in place, or asleep?

But my eyes and mind couldn't resist looking at this floor, which was made up of thousands of rectangular glass cases of people. These lifelike miniature people looked to have been stuck in time. Some had on nightgowns, ready for bed but not sleeping, just standing by the bed, while others could be seen standing at a bus stop, or waiting in line at a store.

Then, I saw her. I closed my eyes so tears wouldn't escape. It couldn't be, but it was — she was in what appeared to be an abandoned house and lying on a mattress on the floor. She was asleep.

I was losing air. Why would Gill have her in one of these glass cases on his floor? I saw her move just a little. She changed positions. Maybe I could get her attention now. I reached to tap on the glass to let her know her daughter was here too, but Sal reached out and bit my hand, just a little. I was about to scream, but Sallemae held my mouth. Then, she whispered, "Do you want to take her place in that glass hell?"

I saw something new in her eyes. It was truth. She was stern and straightforward; They each challenged me in a way they had never challenged me before, with eyes to kill; they had no intention of letting me wake her up.

A powerful force was coming closer to us. It was so strong that when it walked past us, we were pushed backward. Gill entered the room, and fear shook my body. He walked with a slight limp, but he was quick.

We could only see the back of him, but I noticed Gill had a long black cape that looked to be made of kissing snakes. I wanted to see if the snakes were actually coming out of his skull. Was this man a snake? Then he moved the cape to the side of him just a little, and I noticed it was simply a living snake cape. Why didn't the snakes just devour him? They were long anaconda-looking snakes.

Gill picked up a spongelike object and squeezed it, and red stuff dripped into a large wine-type glass. He walked right past us, and I got a full view of the back of him. He was holding the red drink with his long, thick fingernails; was Gill drinking blood?

This man is drinking blood, I thought. *He's not just odd, he's a vampire.* He smelled, I thought, of mothballs. He walked slowly to sit on one of those living chairs made of locusts. He sat before a large black mirror, and I wondered what could he see in that chair. He appeared to be enjoying his drink.

Sallemae was pulling me away. I wanted to knock on the glass before I left, but she was holding my hands. I was thinking to myself, *Wake up people!* I wanted to wake up all of the people in those glass cases. They all looked asleep. Why were they sleeping?

Gill stood up. He was walking much too slowly, and was coming just a little closer, and I wanted to see the front of him. From the back, he did not have a head full of luxurious long black hair. It looked as if he had alopecia and just a small island of hair down the center of his head, like a mohawk.

Sallemae begged me with her eyes to leave, but I couldn't move. The locusts and some of the flies were asleep, but what was that on the side panels of his wall? It looked hard.

One of the eyes of the thing opened, and I noticed it was a lizard, and it wasn't asleep. In fact, this lizard had changed position by one inch. I saw Gill slowly turning his head as the lizard repositioned. I felt pressure in the center of my head as Gill was turning around. A part of me was wanting to see his face, but another lizard opened its eyes, and it was clear Gill was on to something, so I yelled, "Take us home!" right before the lizard and Gill got to see us.

Seconds later, I was back on the beach. Then I yelled, "Take us to the beach mansion!" Now, I was right inside the mansion.

"That was weird," Sal said. She was nervous and sweating. It was as if she'd run ten miles without water.

"I didn't think it was weird. I actually liked it," I said, trying not to show I was scared to my bones and had peed my pants.

That's when Sallemae stood right in my face, eyeball to eyeball.

"I don't care if you liked it or loved it, we ain't ever going back! If you want to go back, you go back by yourself, you got that, little girl?"

Wow, I thought, *big bad words for a girl I can speak death on.* She called me "little girl," which let me know this wasn't a girl my age, although she looked my age—this was a fully grown woman. She was obviously afraid, and she'd obviously meant it.

Now, I'd never backed away from a fight before—just wasn't what we do in my hood. Even if I'd lose the fight, if you got in my face, you got a fight. But this was a lot to take in, Gill's place, and I needed more time to process all of this. So, I did what my mother always told me to do in order to avoid a fight. I walked away.

I sat on my nice Italian leather couch and let her have her moment. Maybe she thinks I'm afraid. She can think that, but all I know is that Gill is not who he appears to be, and somehow, Sallemae is my same height. She grew—we are all now the exact same size and weight. Wonder how that happened.

I moved to the recliner chair and closed my eyes. With much luck, I hoped I wouldn't have to think. Maybe all this was a dream and the next day I would wake up home. Sal and Sallemae were looking intently at me.

"Don't look at me. Turn away," I said. And like toy soldiers, they obeyed.

If I was going to cry (and I just might), they wouldn't see it. And if I cried, it wouldn't be because I was afraid, or that I was weak; if I cried — as I am sometimes capable of doing — it would simply be because I felt alone ... alone in a very strange world.

I cried.

15

WHAT HEROES ARE
MADE OF

The next day came, and I was hungry. So hungry, I spoke up a breakfast bar and ate it. I was wearing the same clothes as the night before, so I can only conclude I slept in my clothes. I saw a fly on the window, and my mind was automatically brought back to Gill's house, which I didn't want to think about. I spoke, "Kill all flies," and a few flies which were obviously in the house fell to the floor.

I wondered if I could speak, "Kill all flies everywhere," and Gill would end up with no chandelier. I smiled and said it anyway. "Kill all flies in Learned Kansan." I smiled because if, in fact, I killed all flies in Learned Kansan, Gill would be wondering what happened to his chandelier around about now. Tons of flies would be falling to the floor and those frogs would be having a field day.

I smiled, but was quickly reminded this was not a laughing matter. The girls were out swimming. I looked out my window and watched as they swam and laughed like we didn't just see a man draped in a snake cape with flies for a chandelier and people in a glass floor. Maybe this was something they were used to in Middle Heaven.

All I really knew was that I had to get out of this. It was this thought that gave me the will to fight. I hadn't really ruled out that all of this could be some episodic dream, waiting for me to bring about the climax. So, here was my first move for a bang-up climax.

The two sisters came back in from a delightful swim. How do I know it was delightful? Sal said it, just as Sallemae reached for the OJ. I calmly said to them, "It's time for you girls to go now."

You would think for one moment time had stopped, or — and this is more likely the truth — that I had shocked them into silence.

"What do you mean, go? Girl, I ain't going *no-where*," said Sallemae.

But that was OK. I had come to expect that from her, for I believed she was the brightest of the two. As much as she liked to believe that she had me down pat with my hand and head movements, she had yet to learn that I don't back down.

"Yes, you are, because this is my mansion, and I want you out!"

"People don't always get what they want, you gon' soon learn that," she said, looking like I'd just taken her candy and she wanted to cry.

"Well, that's not true. In fact, Gill — remember him, the weird dude wearing a snake coat? — well, he told us that we can have whatever we wanted, all we have to do is say it. So, I'm saying it. Go!"

"Where are we supposed to go?" Sal asked, in tears.

However, I wasn't moved by her tears. Stinky had taught me that crying can sometimes mean you are guilty. Besides, the only thing that will move me is being back home on Drake Street. So, I told her, "I don't care where you go. You can jump off a bridge, for all I care."

"That's just mean! *Shhhhhhhh*, don't say no more!" Sal said.

I didn't know exactly why she shushed me, but before I could say another word, they were gathering their few little outfits we picked out together and heading for the door. I really didn't want them to jump off a bridge; it was just a figure of speech. But I'd had enough.

They were stopping me from thinking with all their laughing and talking. It was as if they were sent into my life to stall my time. Reminded me of a sermon my father preached one day titled, "The Distraction," about people who come into your life to distract you from moving on. I didn't need any distractions, especially since I couldn't afford to fail this mission I was on—the mission of getting back home.

For the hours to come, my mind was becoming my greatest distraction. I was thinking about Gill and wondered, *What would have happened to me if I had seen his face?* I couldn't stop thinking about his house and that funky cape he wore.

I hit myself in the head. What was happening to me? My thoughts were on an express train to nowhere. Then, I started to think about the people in my community who were on a mission, and clarity drifted back into place.

I thought about Ms. Nelson, who is on a mission by herself. She makes sure that everyone in the community has photos to remember who they are. When we have a block club party or backyard picnic, she brings her camera and takes pictures, and I don't ever recall her charging anyone for the extra copies she makes and gives to the community.

Mr. B is a hero, sunshine or rain, who is always in the shoe shop serving the old heads a fresh cup of coffee. He could have left that community years ago, but he comes back every day as new and old people alike sit down and talk the local news with him.

My dad shows up at the church three days a week. He is there to baptize our young and old, marry your children, and bury your dead. One thing I have learned about these mission-driven people, they keep showing up, and they simply don't give up. It's because they stay and are consistent that the community is enlightened.

I sat on the floor, more determined than ever. I was staying, and this mission was my mission.

I decided that I would put this mystery together as if I was putting together a puzzle. Purpose came to me. So, here was how I saw it: *stalling time.* That was what all of this was for — giving us all of this stuff was just to stall time! And why would someone want to stall time? So that time could run out and we would be stuck in this place. Maybe that was what Gill wanted. Maybe he was a dream killer, and we would end up in those glass cases anyway.

Oh my! Could it be that after five days there was no return? Would we end up stuck in this place forever? Was that how we could even believe this place was real in the first place?

What if Learned Kansan was just a place where people went and got stuck in their own imaginations, and then lived out their dream over and over again to themselves and other people? After I started allowing my imagination to run a marathon, puzzle pieces were being put together; slowly but surely, I was beginning to understand.

OK, this may be crazy, but what if the people in Learned Kansan got points for getting people to stay? But if they did get points for getting people to stay, what about if they couldn't convince people to stay? What would happen then? If visitors ended up leaving, they would ... suddenly everything inside of me slowed to stillness.

If the people in Learned Kansan didn't get visitors to stay through the five days, they would — of course — be punished! That had to be why they were working so hard at it. Just as I was about to write all of this down and give it to Marion, I heard the doorbell ring.

I ran down the stairs, hoping in my heart that it was the wannabe-me twins or my fake best friends (both names apply to them). Yes, I wanted them back, for now I knew exactly what I would do to get them to talk. It was their irritation that forced — no, demanded — that my brain think outside the norm. So, I swung open the door, and … nope … it was Sharie.

The first thing she did was give me a hug — a hug so tight and real that I knew she finally understood. Then she looked me square in the eye and whispered, "We gotta get out of here, and we only got two days to do it!"

I grabbed her and hugged her again. I think I hugged her for all of five minutes. It felt so good just to have one of the shortiez from the hood believe that I was telling the truth. Someone to just believe! I could hardly breathe, but I had to ask, "What made you finally believe me?"

"Well … Jeffery," she answered. "He didn't say it outright. I don't think he could say it outright. He kept putting all the fun things I wanted to do off until after Saturday. It was like he needed me to stay a little while longer. I started to get suspicious. I told him, 'My friend is right; we've got to get out of here.'

"I thought he would ignore what I said, but he didn't. Then he said, around five minutes later, 'Salle is a pain at times, but do you find that she is oftentimes right?' He just looked at me with tears in his eyes. Then, he told me his replacement was mute and couldn't talk until she got to Learned Kansan. He told me he was blind and couldn't see, and all he ever wanted to do was see again. He did all kinds of evil, destructive things because he couldn't see. It took him receiving eyesight to realize that he already had all he ever needed to be happy.

"I asked where his replacement went, and he said, 'Back home.' He choked, or rather started coughing—he was unable to speak. I wanted more answers, but Jeffery was mute, he couldn't talk. I had the feeling Gill was controlling his speech. This was new to Jeffery because he was holding his ears, and I understand that if you are mute, sometimes you can hear a ringing in your ears which causes you to hold your ears. That must have meant he couldn't say more, but he knew that I knew.

"Now, the way I see it, we are their replacements, and if they get us to stay, they go back home, but if we leave, they have to stay until some lost soul ends up here again. I told him we would do Disney World on Saturday. He smiled, and I told him to go home and then I came right here!

"Salle, this place is real, and we can be trapped here. Jeffery had to leave. I can only assume he was hearing ringing sounds in his ears, which prevented him from hearing and speaking, but he said enough. He was still communicating with me in silence. Because I am mute back home, I have no problem listening in silence and listening through your eyes or emotions."

I told Sharie that she could be right, and there could even be a darker reason we were here. I told her all about Gill's house, the chandelier made out of flies, locusts for furniture, and lizards as side wall paneling, and, although I didn't see the face of Gill, I told her how he looked from the back. She was silent.

I didn't tell her I knew one person who was in the glass floor, because I wasn't sure, and anyway, we had to get out of this place and leave the rescue of the floor people for someone else to do. This was a lot to take in, and I could see Sharie felt overwhelmed. After a long, awkward pause, Sharie looked around my place. Then she said, "Look how you livin', girl! You livin' large!"

"I know, right? And I got clothes from all over the world. I'm styling for real! This is my crib, you dig?"

"I dig!" Sharie exclaimed as she ran upstairs to see the bedroom. "So, where are the silly girls?" Sharie asked.

"Oh, I told them to jump off a bridge."

Sharie looked at me, I guess to search my face for sincerity, and when I didn't crack a smile, she laughed and said, "Girl, you still crazy."

"Yeah, think I inherited that, and Middle Hell can't take that away."

We sat on the edge of the bed and cried. I think we cried for the same reason. If this was really Middle Heaven and not just some sort of extended, bring-your-friend-along-for-free dream, then we were really in this place. The reality was setting in that we could actually get stuck here and never be able to see our family again ... *forever*. In this place, we really didn't know how long forever was, but any time was a long time when all you wanted was just to go home.

We also could have been crying because we were just thirteen-year-old kids. We didn't know what we were up against, and we didn't know what would happen if we couldn't beat this.

"I have a plan," I finally said.

"You do?" Sharie asked excitedly.

"Not really," I admitted, but it had sounded good to be able to say it. What I did know for sure, though, was that nothing moved unless we all moved together, so Sharie and I being alone in that mansion was not the answer. We had to get the boys.

"How many days did you say we had?" I asked.

"Two," Sharie said.

"Then we don't have any time to waste!"

I looked around the luxurious mansion I had always imagined I would live in one day and cursed it. Never again did I want to see the place, and in an instant, we were standing on the grassy lawn, the only trace of the house that remained.

"Why did you do that? Now we've got to live with Stinky," Sharie complained.

She had a point. But us being separated from the boys was not going to get them to see how silly this whole thing was or help us get back home fast.

"So," I said, somewhat unsure, like I was searching for answers to fall that appeared to be stuck in outer space. Still, I managed to say (and I believed this with all my heart), "Maybe that's good we all live together. Maybe with us being there, they will realize this thing we are living is not a dream, but rather, a nightmare."

Sharie looked at me and didn't question my judgment. She just stood up and gave me her hand.

"Let's go," Sharie said, self-determined.

I stood up and gave her my hand, and for once it felt good not to be in control. It felt good to have my friend back.

Then she said something which helped me know Sharie had not changed at all.

"We got some Gill butt to kick."

"Ain't that the truth," I said.

And together, hand in hand, we were off to live with the boys, with every inch of determination a couple of girls could muster up. Gill might be tough, but I guessed it was about time he learned what girl-power-from-the-heart-of-urban-America *tough* really was.

16

TWO KINGS CAN'T RULE

We made it to the hotel room, and it was no surprise to see how the boys were living. We showed up out of the blue, and they didn't even pretend to have anything to hide from us. They were keeping it pretty much the same as our little clubhouse on Drake Street: cookies on the floor, paper cups on the table, half-full cups of punch still sittin' out from the night before, clothes covering the carpet—the place was a mess. One of the managers had given Ryan and Stinky a gift. It was a watch that talked and showed pictures; they could play games on it.

So when Sharie and I showed up, that was what they had to show us first—just like boys, not one time did they think to ask us why we were there.

"Look, Sharie, I bet you ain't got it like *this*," Stinky said with sheer joy.

It is kinda cool, I thought, *but still the perfect little distraction.*

He took out the watch — or whatever it was — and held it up. It looked like he was wearing Liberace's rejected jewelry. That thing had so many fake diamonds it was blinding.

"And watch this: show me a picture of Janet Jackson's boobies," Stinky said.

When he said the word "boobies," Ryan and Marion jumped up and down, covering their mouths, as if that word was still forbidden in this world, or whatever you wanted to call this place.

"I can't do that," the machine said.

"And why not?" asked Stinky.

"You have to be sixteen. You're restricted for the next eight years."

They all laughed hysterically as if this was a good thing. I simply thought it was another toy for another silly boy. Nothing about the thing was amazing to me. I had to act like it, anyway, and Sharie shared my fake sentiments as she didn't crack a smile. We just looked around the place and started doing what we would do as if we were in the clubhouse — we started cleaning.

We threw away plates with old pizza stuck to them, hung up clothes, and cleared off tables, and they pretty much did what they would have done if they were in the clubhouse (which did not include helping us). After some cleaning up, Sharie and I landed on the floor, exhausted, in two separate corners of the room.

We heard a knock on the door. Stinky got engaged enough that he turned off his little new-age machine, gadget box, or whatever you want to call it. Ryan went and opened the door, and two men rushed in. I grabbed the broom, and Sharie grabbed a chair, but before we could do anything, Marion jumped up and kicked one of the guys to the floor, cheered on by Stinky and Ryan. He spun around and did an incredible jump kick to the other guy, who fell to the floor.

The first guy got up, big and sweaty — Asian-looking, but I couldn't be sure, as he wore a mask on one side of his face. He took out a pair of connecting black sticks and went after Marion. Marion jumped over his head, kicked the guy's knees and brought him to the floor, then somehow took the black sticks and choked him to the ground. Two big men who looked to be bodyguards came in and pulled the two unconscious men away.

"Tell them," Marion screamed after them, "there's more where that came from!"

Stinky, Ryan, and the two silly girls all clapped and cheered as Sharie and I just looked at each other like, *This is some bull* – (you know the rest).

Ryan jumped up and raised Marion's arm, saying, "He was the kick-butt king in Chicago, the Bruce Lee of the hood, and he's killing it in this world, too. He's gonna hurt 'em on Saturday." Ryan sat back on the bed and joined Stinky in playing games again.

The word *Saturday* stuck with me because I knew why the fight was set to Saturday. "Pure idiots," I wanted to say, but they were my friends.

Marion went back to watching television with the two teenagers sitting close beside him, one lying on his shoulder. I smiled at him and he gave me a thumbs up. I thought he would still be angry, but he was more concerned with showing off for me than staying mad at me. So, I signaled for Mr. Casanova to come over and talk to me, which he did, telling his two admirers he would be right back.

"They love me," Marion sighed, "I can feel it."

"Sure you can. The question is, *how much* do they love you?"

"I don't care," he said to me pridefully, for it wasn't love that he wanted. He simply wanted eternal attention.

"I know you don't care. I'm just saying, if only the girls back in the hood could see you now."

"I know," he agreed, "that's what I've been screaming! Not just the girls, but the boys, too. Where else but here could I pull two hot teenagers? Hey, you know what I told them?"

"What?" l asked, only half-wanting to know the answer.

"I told them I was in high school and that I was rich back in Chicago, like the Fresh Prince of Bel-Air. They believed me! They believe everything I say. It's incredible!"

"Yeah, considering you can have whatever you say."

I could see that Marion was having the time of his life, but for one second, I caught a glint of concern in his eyes. Maybe I struck a chord. This was something I never even shared with Sharie, but I had done a whole lot of speaking and getting, and it's strange, but after a few days, I felt weird—or maybe not so much *weird*, but more like myself again.

Marion was a sixth-grader. Getting girls way out of his league to buy into his lie must have been exciting, but if he thought for one second those girls didn't see through his lie, he was in for a rude awakening. So, I took the only shot I

179

had open. I had to get him to ask for the prize now, not later, if indeed he was "the man."

So, I whispered, "You should get them to give you that kiss and whatever now. If you're such a man, why you got to wait for later? I mean, you really want bragging rights when we leave this place? Why won't they go all the way?"

"Well," he said, confused, "the computer gadget—watch box?—that machine thing told them I wasn't ready and that I had to wait three more years. Maybe they know I'm not ready."

"You? Not ready?" I asked in fake disbelief. "Look at you! You are Kick-Butt Marion, here *and* in Chicago. Besides, they believed your story about being rich back home. What's not ready about you? Look, Marion, you only got two days to enjoy this. Why are they making you wait? Don't you get it? Maybe they're tricking you, playing you!"

In total disbelief, shaking his head "no" relentlessly, he began to pace the floor. It was at this point I knew I had him; he was breaking. I knew I had to get him back over to the girls to go for it, and I equally knew they weren't going to because that would defeat their purpose, which was to distract him until Saturday. So, I pressed in even harder. "Go! Go for it now; don't wait. Who's the man?"

"I'm the man," he said, somewhat unsure.

"Well, then prove it."

I watched as the thirteen-year-old boy went over to get his kiss from the two swooning teenagers. I picked up a magazine with a picture of Stinky and Ryan — or I should say, "Rain Man and Thunderbolt" — on the cover holding a lot of cash. Man, these cats down here in this fake music business sure knew how to make a dream big. I laughed as I began to read the article titled, "If My Friends Could See Me Now."

Meanwhile, Sharie was sitting on the bed talking to Stinky, asking him how he felt on that stage. Stinky was all too free to talk while Ryan was simply lying on the bed. Ryan was pretending he wasn't listening, but Sharie and I both knew that he was. She was really playing into Stinky's ego, and he was giving her an earful.

"So, tell me, Stinky, how did it feel, I mean *really* feel, to be on that stage?"

"It was like magic — all the people clapping and girls fainting. Did you see the girls fainting?"

"I think I did. Actually, I think I saw the same girl faint."

"What you mean?" Stinky asked naively.

181

"I mean, I think the same girl fainted at both concerts. Was she wearing a red sweater?"

"And black pants," Stinky recalled.

"That's her, the same girl. She fainted at both concerts."

"She must be a really big fan of mine to come two days straight to the same concert and faint at the same time. I'm the *man*!"

At this point, Ryan interrupted. "She was fainting for me; I was the headliner," Ryan said, sure of himself.

"I was the headliner, too," Stinky argued. "They're my fans, too. Didn't Moochie tell you we share fans?"

Now Ryan was out of his seat and up in Stinky's face. "Again, that girl was my fan! She dyed her hair red. My fans are the redheads, like me."

"Calm down," Sharie said. "I mean, both of you guys rock."

Stinky looked at Sharie. "Just like when he's in Chicago," he muttered. Then he said more loudly, "Ain't it strange that Sharie's talking? I always wondered what she would sound like if she could talk."

"Me too," Ryan agreed.

"What's that got to do with anything?" Sharie snapped back.

I cleared my throat because I didn't want Sharie to get into her feelings. She had them going at each other, something about the concert was becoming a reality, and I needed her to push in on it. She got me, just like she always did when we were in Chicago. She understood this was it; this is what it was going to take to break down these two pinheads.

"I mean," Sharie added in a much calmer tone, "I mean, what you should wonder is how these same girls gon' faint at the same time, wearin' the same clothes. Who does that? If I had the chance to meet, let's say — "

"*Jeffery!*" Stinky interrupted. "What happened to that dude?"

"Nothing. We are going to Disney World on Saturday," Sharie answered.

"Oh, cool," Stinky said, and for a moment Sharie had his undivided attention, so she jumped right back into the conversation.

"OK, when I see Jeffery again, I am not going to be wearing the same clothes and doing the same thing at the same time. I mean, who does that?"

"My fans," said Stinky.

"*My* fans," corrected Ryan.

They looked at each other, and although they didn't say anything, you could tell their minds were working.

Sharie was wise enough to let them have their own awakening moment, so she started cleaning up some more, looking back ever so slightly to make sure they were still thinking. These two "kings" could afford much in this world, but an ego was far too costly. I was sure their egos would eventually bring these boys to their knees.

I looked back over at Marion, who was now getting angry because the girls weren't going for it—they wouldn't kiss him before Saturday. They gave every excuse, from wanting it to be something special, to wanting it to be in a special place that wouldn't be available until Saturday, to finally claiming they were nuns and it was going to take them forty-eight hours to disavow their oaths to God.

Marion was a smart guy. I knew he had to see their game. He looked back at me and told them to give him a few minutes. He came over to me and sat on the table. I didn't rub it in. It wasn't the *"I got it!"* moment I had hoped for, but rather, I comforted him in my silence.

Marion looked at me and said, "When do we leave?"

I smiled. *Two more to go.* Then I told him quietly, "Dismiss them. Tell them you don't want to see them anymore."

"Is that what happened to your friends?"

"Well, ah—"

"What have we done, Salle?"

"I don't know, but as for my friends, I think they could be jumping off a bridge," I said.

He smiled.

"How long do we have, Salle?"

"I don't have all the answers, but one thing's for sure. We've got to leave before Saturday, or we could be stuck here."

"For how long?" Marion said with a bowed head and spirit, for it was obvious he was sickened that he had succumbed to the fantasy world.

I looked at him and knew I didn't have to tell him how long; he knew. He got it. He was on board.

"I didn't want to say anything early because I wanted this to be just a nice break from reality like everyone else did," said Marion quietly. "But I noticed something. Each time I spoke, 'I want to be a professional body with powerful a powerful punch and kick' ... well, when these jokers first came for the battle, I was superfast and kicked butt. I felt nothing when I was hit or

185

fell. But this last fight, when I was hit, I felt it, and when I fell down, it hurt—really badly. This place is one big mistake. It's all going to end, I mean."

He went back and told the girls to go home, a car would be waiting for them. He told them he needed time to think of a good surprise for them for Saturday. They were so happy that they even stopped giving me the evil eye. When they left, Sharie, Marion, and I huddled on the far side of the room. Ryan looked at us as if he could read our minds, but he didn't say anything.

Instead, he addressed Stinky: "Stinky-Man, we got a show at the mall tomorrow morning, let's get some sleep."

The two kings went to bed in the same clothes they performed in.

"How we gon' get those two jerks to come aboard?" Marion asked.

"I don't know yet," I answered.

Indeed I didn't, but we only had, to my estimation, a day—at most, a day and a half—to be out of here. Even if we had to drag them headfirst, tomorrow afternoon we were leaving Learned Kansan.

They all drifted off to sleep—well, at least that's how it appeared.

Things were quiet in this world, but although I wasn't sure, I had a feeling neither Stinky nor Ryan was asleep. A couple of hours later, I heard a rattling in the sheets as Ryan was waking up Stinky. I thought I should say something, but something inside of me told me to be still, very still.

"Hey, Stinky," Ryan whispered. I thought it sounded a lot like hissing instead of talking.

"What, man? I got to get my beauty sleep," said Stinky.

"Don't you find it strange that Sharie and Salle are sleeping in *our* room tonight?"

Now Stinky was up and alert.

"Yeah, I find it strange. Wanna kick them out?"

"I can't kick out my cousin," Ryan said, and for one moment, I was glad we were family.

"I think I know why she's here," Ryan said.

"Why's that?" Stinky asked innocently.

"She always trying to save the day, or maybe, and this is just a maybe, but maybe she wishes *she* was the star."

Now there are not many times I've wanted to choke Ryan, but this was one of them. I will most certainly rule the world, but it won't be as a superstar. Now, I have a killer voice, if I put my mind to it, and I guess one could say I'm all-

187

out talented, but I don't want to be a star—nope not me. I could always marry one, but me dancing around on stage for attention wasn't my dream, and as often as Ryan and I talked, he should have known this. But I listened anyway, hoping against my better judgment to hear something that could redeem these two kings. Then, Stinky sat up, as if he had the world's greatest new idea.

"I think that's it!" Stinky almost shouted, only to be hushed by Ryan using his hand to cover his mouth.

"She's always trying to sing and stuff knowing she doesn't know how. I'm just saying, we could be living *her* dream," Stinky said.

"I know," said Ryan, "I thought about that, but she's always the one who sort of saves our butts, and she *is* pretty smart—and I'm not just saying that because she's my cousin."

"Well, maybe *we* should save the day," said Stinky.

I really wanted to interject and say, "Boy, you can't save twenty-five cents, how can you save a day?" but I didn't. We had less time than I'd thought, and I was praying that these clowns would get it right, so I shut my eyes tight.

"How we gonna do that?" asked Ryan.

"I think I got it!" Stinky jumped up.

"Don't be so loud! What is it?" said Ryan.

"I'm going to save the day because I got it! Remember how we were supposed to do that challenge? Ten good things, remember? I was thinking that's the reason this world feels so strange to me."

"So you do feel it," Ryan said.

"Feel what?" repeated Stinky.

"Strange," said Ryan.

"A little—well, a lot strange, like a 'sometimes I feel someone is living in my body, and I'm just watching them' strange; and low-key, that dude Gill creeps me out," Stinky said.

"Man, I wish Marion would knock that dude out for me," Ryan said.

"Me too!"

"But I don't think we can speak anything against him, though."

"Why would you say that?" Ryan asked

"Well, I wished him to fall down the stairs. Remember when he yelled at us?"

"At you," Ryan corrected.

"OK, he yelled at me and I wished him to accidentally trip down the stairs. Well, it was only two stairs. But he looked back at me and smiled. He knew. Anytime we wish things about him, he hears it, I think. He's just weird, right?"

"Right weird," said Ryan.

They gave each other a high five.

"But I think I got it," said Stinky. "Maybe if we did the ten good things, we could all just leave and Salle could get off our backs or whatever," said Stinky.

"That's brilliant," said Ryan.

No, it's not, I thought, but the challenge *had* been lost in all this mess. Could Stinky be on to something? I was now totally in tune with their solution.

"Let's just do the ten good things now," said Ryan. "We are all here, so it's still the group. We're just doing all the work".

"OK, watch this." Stinky got up and put on his computer watch thingy (or whatever you call it) and spoke into it: "Hey, lady, we have been given the challenge to do ten good things. Can you track this for me?"

The computer spoke back: "Yes, I can, would you like me to store it in your memory folder?"

"I would," Stinky continued. "Hey, can you sign each good thing that I do, too?"

"I can. Do you need suggestions for good things you could do?" the computer replied.

"No, we got this," said Stinky.

So Ryan and Stinky got dressed and set on the task of doing ten good things. They first picked up clothes off the floor, then they straightened out the pillow under Sharie's head and covered me with a blankie.

I wanted to say, "That's not a good thing, I'm hot," but I didn't want to stop this. I didn't think it was the answer, but the boys were becoming aware of something, and that was the most important thing. They cleared off the table, cleaned the bathroom's tub and sink, put shoes in boxes, and gave each other compliments.

It was almost comical: the clowns actually thought that us just being in the room counted as us being a part of it. They opened the door and gave the guard some old food, and later on, gave him clothes for a family member. Finally, with nothing else to do, they cleared off the television and dusted the room.

Stinky, feeling proud of himself, sat on the bed and was joined by Ryan.

"Computer lady, how many good things have we done so far?" Stinky asked.

"Eleven good things, all signed and saved in your storage—and my name is *Cookie*," the computer lady replied with firm annoyance.

"We did more than ten good things," replied Ryan.

"I knew we could do it," chuckled Stinky.

"Still feels sort of strange," said Ryan.

191

"I guess so," said Stinky.

I felt sorry for the boys and sorrier for myself. Maybe this was a dream to them, and maybe I didn't really want to sing, and maybe they were not "bad luck charms" as I'd often called them in the past. Maybe they were just bad kids because they had little else to do. I didn't want to work with them at all. I'd rather just let me and Sharie complete the challenge. But, if nothing else, when I got back home, I thought maybe I'd start looking at them differently.

With the boys almost asleep, Stinky had just one more question, the one question he knew Ryan would appreciate him asking.

"Computer lady — oops, Cookie — when will I see my mother?" Stinky asked.

The computer replied, "Negative."

"Negative?" repeated Ryan, "What does that mean?"

"I don't know," said Stinky. "Negative can be good, right?"

"Let me ask, maybe your computer is just tired."

Ryan went and got his wrist computer, and now I was up and alert. Could this computer know the answer we all sought? All I needed Ryan to do was ask about Chicago, or simply when we would leave Learned Kansan. Ryan turned on his computer and asked, "When will I see Chicago?"

The computer replied, "Negative."

"That makes no sense," replied Ryan. "OK, maybe this will work: how long will I stay in Learned Kansan?"

The computer replied, "Indefinitely."

"Oh," said Ryan, "Indefinitely."

"You know what that word means?" asked Stinky.

"Not really, but we gotta get some sleep tonight."

Both Ryan and Stinky laid down to rest as the word *indefinitely* tried unsuccessfully to find a place in their vocabulary.

17

DON'T HATE ... CELEBRATE

We were awakened by the sound of a familiar voice; it was Gill, the supposedly nice tour guide. He ushered in a group of new stylists and they went straight to Stinky and Ryan. When he walked past me, I felt a kick to the back of my legs which almost made me topple over. Yet Gill looked straight forward, never letting our eyes meet.

I thought to myself, *I can do anything, right?* So, in my head I decided that I would slap that prideful face. I looked to see what would happen, yet it appeared that he didn't feel anything. Then I mumbled under my breath, "Slap Gill." He moved slightly back, as if he knew what I had commended, but he didn't say a word. He just stood in the center of the room, demanding his space to voice his opinion.

Gill brought the news that after the show, the boys had an international television interview.

That caused Stinky and Ryan to jump up and down on their beds as if their beds were trampolines. Gill actually had to make them stop, which was fun to watch because I knew what he had on his hands. They were still the same out-of-control blockheads from Chicago who were a part of my best friend group.

Marion's girls came in, but they were dressed much more outrageously. It was sickening to watch; he was only *thirteen*. I guess a lot can happen to a boy at thirteen. We were from the hood, and for boys from the hood, thirteen is the year for discovery. To my surprise, they kissed Marion. Actually, it surprised us all.

"What was that about?" I said, hoping that this statement would embarrass the girl groupies. They looked so much older than a thirteen-year-old kid, and I know their mama didn't give them permission to dress like that and kiss teenage boys in strange hotel rooms.

"Oh, nothing, we just think he is great!" one of the groupies responded.

I looked at Marion, hoping he could see the lie in that statement, hoping he knew that greatness didn't befall a person overnight, and hoping against hope that he was still glued to the truth and was still on our side.

Gill asked about Jeffery, and Sharie explained to him that they were planning a trip to Disney World in a few days, which seemed to please him. He looked at me but didn't speak or ask any questions. I was slightly disappointed. I really wanted to tell him I had told my girls to go jump off a bridge. Of course, I didn't want them to die (if that was even possible). Hopefully, they found a parachute. But jump they must! I smiled to myself.

Gill looked back and smiled as if I had just said something that amused him. I didn't think he could read minds, but what I felt he was really good at was reading one's motivation, or maybe he could interpret actions and facial expressions. I think the two fake friends he gave me had a little of that power, which is why I have learned that in this place, the best thing to think is nothing—always do the unexpected.

The boys' room, or should l say *the superstars'* room, started to fill with people of various duties. One person focused on clothes while another person did hair. I couldn't help but notice all the fancy products they were using to slick Ryan's hair back. My eyes drifted to the person putting out nice jelly rolls, milk, and orange juice. As I stuffed my face with rolls and dried nuts, Gill came close enough for me to smell his cologne.

"Old Favor?" I asked.

He looked at me with eyes that could kill but managed to smile a crooked smile and say, "Well, yes, it is, as a matter of fact."

He walked away, swinging his arms as if I had just offended him or something. Maybe he was mad he'd woken up with no chandelier. Or maybe I was on to something he didn't want me to know? It gave me something else to think about, another little take on this place.

What "young" man around Gill's age would be caught dead wearing Old Favor? My father wouldn't even wear that cologne. However, it's my grandfather's favorite. Well, Mr. Gill, I never trusted you in the first place, but now I really don't trust you. I suspect this is a front: If only I could have gotten a closer look at your face in that place you call a home. My guess is that you are around sixty-five, and you may be a million years old. Too bad I didn't see the front of you.

At first, I thought I was hearing things. It sounded like voices—my voice, actually—coming from the hotel hallways. They were talking to Gill, and he seemed pleased

Sal said, "So sorry we are late, but Bridge Street was three cities away."

Sallemae added, "Who knew we didn't have a Bridge Street in Learned? Strange." Before I could blink twice, standing before me and looking a lot like me were Sallemae and Sal. They were even wearing the same outfit I had on; now how did they know that? Well, they *did* act like me, and that was both flattering and irritating, but mostly flattering. I'd always thought my style was good enough to be copied. But I didn't like seeing them. The only reason they could be back was to stop the plan.

"I thought I told you girls to go jump off a bridge," I said boldly.

Sallemae's smile was much too cheerful to be genuine. "Girl, we know you didn't mean to kill us, so we searched for hours until we found a Bridge Street east of Wisconsin, and we jumped off the curb. So, technically we did jump off a bridge—off of Bridge Street."

Had I just heard what I thought I heard? Clever, how they saved their pathetic behinds. Actually, very clever. With as much anger as I could muster, I shouted, "Get away from me!"

I stressed the "*me*" part.

They moved a short distance, but still close enough for me to hear them speak: "I think you may want to take that back. I have a feeling you are going to need us," Sal said tearfully.

"How about I. Will. Never. Need. You."

"How about," Sallemae whispered to me, "I know you want to leave this place and you're going to need someone to show you the way, and it ain't going to be Gill, so you better cool it, girl."

"Come closer," I demanded. "Why should I trust you?"

Sal dropped her cupcake. I leaned down to help her pick it up and she whispered, "I don't know how much you know, but when we get a break in the concert, I'll tell you everything. It's not about you now, it's about us. We don't have long."

"I know, one day."

"No," Sal corrected me, "you have about twelve hours. When we get to the concert, let's talk, but we cannot let Gill know. He will stop it, and he is powerful."

I still didn't know that I should trust them, so I said again, and this time a little louder, "How do I know I can trust you?"

Then Sallemae whispered in my ear, "Feeling a little weaker now, are you? Things not coming as fast as they used to come, are they? Most people never noticed. We didn't. But you start to feel like yourself again. You know what it feels like to feel human? I would give anything to just feel that again ... So, if you don't trust me, who are you going to trust?"

She got up and Gill was looking right at us. He walked over, looking angrily at Sallemae, and asked, "What did you tell her?"

"Nothing!" Sallemae lied.

I didn't know why she was helping us, but for the moment, I was glad someone was. I slipped Marion and Sharie a note telling them to stay near the back dressing room because twelve hours was all we had.

Gill was calling us to get in the car; the boys had to be at the mall. We all separated into whatever cars were available, but it wouldn't be for long. I made sure I got in the car with the two little boys just in case I had to drag them along the way because we were leaving this place and they were going with us even if we have to drag them by the hair. Trust me, wouldn't be a pretty sight, but it would get done. Can you say, "Bye-bye Learned Kansan?" Well, I can, and soon.

18

"THE COLOR IS RED"

As they were ushered to the stage area, I stayed near, so close I could hear Moochie telling the audience how this up-and-coming group was taking the nation by storm. Next, the audience would see a little video about how this all got started.

Stinky was signing a few autographs from a couple of young girls around his age who had somehow made a pathway to the back area. They stood with their mother. Stinky signed their autographs and said, "Is that your mother?"

One girl flirtatiously looked at Stinky and said, "Yes, it's cool that my mom is so cool, she likes you guys as well."

"Yeah, it is cool," said Stinky. "I have a cool Mom too."

The girls walked away, excited to be holding a piece of paper with Stinky's name on it. When they walked away, Stinky turned away from me. Sending those girls over to stroke Stinky's ego may not have been the thing to do, and I was glad Gill had thought it necessary to do, for what may have happened is that Gill just made Stinky miss his mother. Good looking out, Gill, good looking out.

Ryan walked over next to me. I could just tell something had been bothering Ryan, so I went for it and asked, "Ryan, are you cool?"

Ryan looked at Stinky and didn't answer right away. "He is enjoying this, you know," said Ryan. "Here he is more than just that smelly kid."

"I know."

That's all I could bring myself to say: "I know." *Maybe that's a good thing,* I thought. My grandpa, whom I always thought was a cracked egg—well, anyway he would always say, "When an egg cracks a little, cook the whole egg." I think—well, I'm not really sure—but I think he always meant that when things are in motion, just let it happen. Let it crack.

Time was ticking. These could be our last hours before we were trapped here. My only hope was that Ryan would pick up on this and that he wouldn't gamble. He and Stinky were the only ones left to realize this place was not all it was cracked up to be. Ryan, treading on thin ice, moved Stinky a little closer to the curtain.

I moved nearer. I wanted to hear, but not be rude.

Ryan whispered, "Hey, Stinky, what if this place is just some evil alter-world that traps us after five days and we are here indefinitely, which I am pretty sure means a very long time?" Ryan asked.

It was as if he'd opened up a fire hydrant. The once-bold Stinky turned into a well of tears. In a frantic cry, he said, "That's what I've been thinking! We gotta get out of here, right now! Let's go. My mamma needs me."

"Wait, calm down!" Ryan warned. "Let's see if the same girl in the red top faints again at the same time during the concert. If she does, we run off the stage and we keep running until we are out of this building. Got that?"

"OK, I got it," Stinky said, drying his eyes. "I wanna go home."

"Me too. I was only staying because of you," admitted Ryan.

"The only reason I was staying was because of you!" said Stinky.

They hugged each other, then, realizing this was not normal for them in their relationship, they quickly pulled apart and gave each other high fives. I was happy, and my heart felt like a hundred pounds had been lifted. We were finally all on the same page.

"Remember," said Ryan, "the girl in red."

"Got it," said Stinky.

Gill walked backstage to see why they hadn't run out on the stage yet. Stinky was supposed to do three flips, but now he would only have time for two. The show was going as normal — the crowd was large and excited and the music was loud. The only difference was that the two boys on stage weren't looking for applause this time, but for the girl in red. If she fainted, and I was sure she would, they would run.

Meanwhile, Marion and Sharie were standing in a huddle in a small private area near the door. I ran over excitedly and gave them a thumbs-up. I didn't want to be heard.

Sal and Sallemae came back and joined our circle as if they were on our side.

"OK, why are you two here," I said. I knew it wasn't nice, but I wasn't trying to be nice.

Sallemae said, "Well, I think you want us here."

"Ahhhh … let me think," I said. "No, I don't think we want you here, but if you got something we need to hear, say it and run along. Time is limited."

It was sort of surprising to me that Sal took the lead; that was not her style. She was always messing up things. But she took a deep breath as if she has been waiting a long time to simply exhale, then she explained.

"We came here from New York many years ago. So many, I don't think I remember. We were best friends, but we always wanted to be someone else. We were instigators mostly, but we had big dreams in a town known for taking bits out of people. The portals were open in certain places in New York, and we got our wish. We were different celebrities for five whole days. Now, don't get me wrong, you still get a lot of advantages living out here—no crime, free housing, and of course, jobs all over the place, but this becomes your life. You don't keep the ability to speak things into existence. You become just like everyone else: regular working-class people. Whatever you don't think about, you won't miss—until one day, you want to go back home. Then you may have a problem.

"That's dumb," Sharie said. "What about your family?"

"Well …" Sal cleared her throat. "The people who guided us became us—nothing like us being you. Guess it took us a while to learn this. When they trade places, they have a small amount of time to learn your mind and habits. Most do. Lots of people from the underworld are living in our world. I mean, if people get suspicious, the replacements can be called back to this world and maybe you'd go back, I'm not sure. Anyway, I guess our replacements nailed it. There's one more way we can go back, but we can't go back to our old lives. I don't think we can ever do that."

OK, my name is Salle with an E, and I usually pick things up quickly, but this all was just one large mess. "OK, maybe I'm missing something, but why should we help you?"

"Wait a minute," Marion said, "I think I get it. It's like trading places. Now that they lost the opportunity to become us, the best they can hope for now is to simply go back home."

"Well, it's not that easy," said Sal, "because you figured it out. Now we all can go back—not back to our old life, but just back to our state and maybe our old professions. But there's nothing like feeling human again! Have you ever heard the phrase everyone has a twin? The person from the underworld is my twin."

"Am I the only one not getting this?" I asked. "We have Ryan, and he's good with maps. I think we can find our way without them!"

"No," said Sal, "Let's put it this way: there are thousands of people who beat the rules but didn't make it out. They became too much of a risk to live here, so they either live as an outcast here or live in a glass case. We don't have a map or anything, but I can assure you we know so much more than you know. We have lived here for years—trust me, we are your best hope."

Marion moved me over to the side and whispered in my ear. "Look, Salle, we don't have time for mistakes. I am so sorry we didn't figure this out sooner, but I think we may need their help."

I just didn't want them with us. It was as if I could hear their thoughts and they could hear my thoughts. I couldn't explain it to Marion, but yeah, some of what they were saying was true— I heard that before they spoke it—but something was not. I just didn't know the "not" part, so I said to them, "What happens to you in this world if we successfully make it back?"

Sallemae and Sal looked at each other and, rather conveniently, Sal said. "We go into glass cases or we die."

"So you die," said Marion, somewhat confused.

"Now he's getting it," said Sal. "Which is why we've got to get you back to that wall. It's not just you needing to get back. We need to get back as well."

I didn't really buy it, but there was a lot about this world I didn't buy or understand. It almost felt as if they were making up this stuff on the go. It was too sloppy with cookie-cutter answers, everything just made to fit in a moment. We looked at each other, and I could tell we all had questions. Now the question was, who would ask them first?

Sharie started the questions, and there were more to follow. "How did we get chosen?"

Sallemae answered, "That's Gill's world that does the choosing. I can tell you guys were the youngest, with the exception of Jeff—he came to us young as well. Jeff was a really hard kid, just always angry."

I looked at Sharie and could tell she disagreed with that statement, but knowing Sharie as I do, I knew she wouldn't voice that disagreement.

"So," said Marion, "It is Gill controlling this whole experiment."

"Well," said Sallemae, "Gill is from the world below. They live amongst us. I don't know their full agenda. I know they have one. It is something we have that they have yet to control or duplicate. All I can tell you is that they are mystical. They can control minds, but not actions. They can create illusions so strong people have killed themselves believing."

I had seen the glass floor. I knew a few people who were trapped here, so I wondered how much would she know and I said, "How many people are here from this strange world?"

Sal answered, "Lots of people. I don't know the total. After a while, it becomes a way of life. Some people have been here so long, they have forgotten who and where they came from. They can control time. I mean, Gill, I think, has lived in every century, that man is so smart."

It was strange, almost like I could hear their thoughts before they spoke them, and I knew most of what they said was true, but for some reason, they were holding back on Gill's identity. So, I asked again.

"Where is this Gill from?"

"Well, we are from your world," said Sallemae. "Let's just say he's not."

So I asked, "Can he just end this right now", is our plight useless?

"NO," said Sal, and she said it without thinking, so I knew it was the truth. "He can't violate rules either. This is a world ruled by laws, and the underworld—wherever he is from—had laws, too. It's something these people need to survive. They can live in our world as parasites, but without us, they die. If not, they would have killed us all off a long time ago. Just know, they are everywhere, and I do mean everywhere."

Marion said, "I think what she is trying to say is that his power is limited, I guess. We have something his world doesn't have or hasn't figured out yet, but there are some things that have got to be your choice. It's like that. Remember, what we were learning in chapel. We have choice, but God is all-powerful. I think it's like that."

OK, I oddly agreed. Gill had weaknesses, we just didn't know them, and that was where I thought these girls might help us out the most. The only surprise was that this statement came from Marion. Now don't get me wrong, even in our world, Marion was good at putting things together. He knew at times how to get us into a situation and how to get us out. I just wasn't used to him being so on point, but this was a new world, and emotions were heightened.

We looked at each other and the hopelessness that lay in the pits of our stomachs had to be ignored. I looked at the girls, tired and just wanting my pillow.

"So," I said, rather exhausted, "simply put, we need you ..."

"OK, simply put, we need each other," said Sallemae.

I could live with that. The only thing I wanted was to get out of here, and as I scanned the faces of my two closest friends, I could tell they were thinking the same things.

I looked at the girls and asked, "What is the timeline?"

"Around ten hours and time is ticking," Sal said.

That was the truth. I knew that we had less time than first imagined.

"Where's Gill?" Sharie asked.

"Oh, he's hovering over the show, making sure if anyone speaks anything bad about the show, he can quickly reverse it," said Sal.

It was almost like Sal had read my mind. I was just about to speak all light off on the stage. I guess as long as the boys agreed the show had to go on.

Sallemae admitted that the performance was all staged or mirrored to look like there were more real fans than were actually there. But what was real was the boys on that stage. This was all one big role you never stop playing.

Finally, I asked the last and most important question: "Could we ever get home without the wall?"

"No," said Sallemae. "The wall is a magnetic portal. You can only go back through a magnetic portal. Unless you came here from I-80. Not everyone here is on assignment."

I found it hard to believe people really chose to live here and intermingle with the perfect people.

We could hear the cheering getting louder for Rain Man and Thunderbolt. This clued us in to where they were at in their show, so we all headed out toward the back door so we'd be standing near the door when the boys came off the stage. This day, if they fought this decision, we will carry them home.

We were all sort of angrily sobered, feeling tricked. This was all one clever deception, and now it was over. But with that anger came a sense of empowerment and anxiety. We had to get out of here! There was a loud commotion, and we all looked at each other, not remembering any type of noise like this in the first show. Suddenly, Stinky and Ryan, torn clothes and all, came running down the hallway. Out of instinct, Marion opened the door just as they ran out.

Ryan looked back at us and shouted, "What are you guys waiting for? We gotta get out of here!"

We all sped out the back door into the parking lot and realized we had no car. We all shouted "Car!" and a small car appeared. We all shouted "Van!" and I added "Driver!" and we all jumped into the van that appeared. Stinky, out of breath and crying, held on to his brother, Marion. We were going somewhere, but we didn't know where. All we knew is we had to get away from Gill.

"What's the matter?" Marion asked.

"The girl ... the girl in red, she fainted at the same time in every show!" Stinky gasped.

So, they had figured it out. It was all just one big game of make-believe.

"Go to the forest preserve," Sallemae instructed. "We can hide from Gill and his crew there. That way we can think and plan."

We had no other plan, so we headed to the nearest forest preserve to give us time to figure out what to do next. In a few seconds, we were at the forest preserve. After Ryan and Stinky changed clothes, we looked like regular kids

215

from Drake Street. We were together again, and now it was time to kick some Gill butt.

19

THE WAY HOME

We wished the car and the driver away — I wasn't too sure they were on our side. We changed into comfortable street clothing, with comfortable shoes. It was a little before two o'clock in the afternoon, and we had until 9 p.m. to get back to the wall. That was a whole seven hours. The twins stated it would take at least six hours, depending on if we would need to detour.

There was a small ravine in the preserve and we started walking along the side of it. Marion put camouflage mud on his face; he was truly into Boy Scout mode. We sat on a large rock and waited until our fear allowed us to speak.

"We need to get back to the place where we started from, where the beautiful stone wall aligned with that stunning blue lake. The wall was around there — I think I saw mountains," Sharie said, pointing.

"I thought I saw trees, like near the water," I added.

Marion said, "I saw a baseball diamond, so it's got to be toward more of a city field."

Then Ryan chimed in. "I saw a cabin, a wood cabin like my grandpa use to take me to when I was younger."

"It's like an open field, near the lake. It's right around the corner from there or something like that," said Stinky.

We looked at each other. It was strange — we all saw different things. We were so taken by the beauty of this place we'd never stopped to compare what we were looking at. Could it have all been an illusion and we were simply at the back of Gill's house? At this point, my antennas came up, and I wondered why we even needed Sallemae and Sal.

"Maps to get back to Earth, home, Chicago," I said out loud.

What appeared was a small map outlining every place we had been and where we needed to go. Ryan, who was a map whiz, looked carefully over the map and defined three routes we could take to get back to an open wall. I looked at the twins and asked which one they thought was the quickest. After carefully reviewing the map, they both decided that we should go to the wall east of the ravine. It was about forty minutes from where we were and we decided that we could walk it.

"Wait a minute," Sharie objected. "Let's leave the girls. We can find this location ourselves."

Thank you, I thought, glad that I wasn't the only one who was thinking along this line.

"But what if we get lost? We can wait to dump them when we see the light from the wall," suggested Marion.

"Wait a minute!" said Sal. "Don't forget that it is to our benefit that you find that wall. The two of us could die. We'll go all the way to make sure we get you there or we won't go at all."

"I don't think you have bargaining chips," I reminded Sal. But we didn't have time to waste, so we were off to find the wall east of the ravine with only five hours left.

20

ON THE MOVE

Although we were all empowered with our own survival energy, our feet had to move faster than our wandering minds. We didn't have time for regret or personal emotional moments; we had to move! And move we did, crashing through tall grass and wooden branches that made their own crackly music.

We were covered in dust and tree branches, and we didn't have the time to keep speaking cleanness on ourselves just to find that we were dirty again. At first, it was just a rustling through the trees, but then we saw a glowing light, and as we moved on, the light became clearer and closer.

"He's watching us! Gill!" I shouted. "I can feel that energy, the same thing I felt in his house. Why is he watching us?"

"The house?" Marion asked.

"Long story. The question is, why is he watching us?"

The boys all looked at me, and I looked at the twins.

"You are his project, remember? He can see you, but he can't stop you," Sallemae responded.

"Wait a minute, do you still have that thing, that watch-computer thingy? Where is it?" I asked Stinky.

Stinky felt his pocket and noticed it was still with him. He took it out and stomped it into the ground.

"I've never seen one of those!" shouted Sal.

Marion came so close to Sal that he could have kissed or killed her, but he said, "You lie one more time, and I will speak you out of existence." We were proud of him, and if it wasn't for time's sake, we all would have hugged him, but we had to move.

We carried on into the woods, the cooing of pigeons guiding the way. I thought about home and how mad my mother was going to be at me for getting into this situation in the first place. It had all started because two boys had decided to cook the science lab.

So, as I moved, I begin to imagine what each of them was thinking. I bet the little one with the short little legs who was leading the pack was thinking he couldn't wait to get back to the place where he was just a kid again, not a celebrity — the place where he could explore his world again with destructive curiosity.

His partner in crime was moving right in stride with him, only steps behind him. I just bet Ryan was thinking about his mother, pets, and train sets; they were moving with speed to get back to the place they knew.

We each carried the burdens and delights of being back home again in our hearts as our feet moved and moved — until Sharie needed a water break.

"Water," Sharie requested, out of breath, but nothing happened. "Water." This time when she said it, it sounded like she was whispering.

I shouted, "Give us water!"

We found a clear stream and sat down on some rocks. Ryan took out the map and informed us that we were only about ten minutes away.

"Ten minutes to home. Praise the Lawwd!"

That was Stinky, always throwing around religious phrases — things that he'd heard from his grandmother 'cause he never went to church much himself. On the few occasions he had to gone to chapel, he slept.

223

"I guess we can take ten more minutes," Marion said as he sat down, removed his shoes, and rubbed his feet.

"Looks like we're in a different place," said Ryan. We each sat down and drank water. Ten minutes was not a long time considering we had been running for thirty-five minutes already. It was getting darker and the sun was not as hot. We heard footsteps in the leaves moving quickly toward us. Stinky jumped up.

"Gill, go away, go away!" he shouted.

We all looked up, armed with the power to speak and the heart to wish his very death if we had to, for Gill was the only person we really feared in this world. He had the most to gain by keeping us here. However, what moved from behind the trees wasn't Gill, or Moochie, or even one of the many goons who were attached to him. It was *Jeffery*, looking like he hadn't even walked a mile, so we knew he was a plant.

"Look at his clothes, Sharie," I warned. "He's a plant."

"No, we can't say that yet," Sallemae said.

There was something about the twins still bothering me. It felt as if they were also watching us, even though they were helping us find and follow the path.

"No one knows I am here, not even Gill," Jeffery said.

"Then why are you here?" Sharie asked.

"I don't know, really. I guess I just wanted to see you."

They looked at each other, and I looked at Sharie. It was clear she still had feelings for him and that was the last complication we needed.

"Well, that's all good, Romeo, but really, we got to keep moving," said Marion as he began to put his shoes back on, gearing up to move out.

"Guys, in ten minutes we'll reach the wall. Just give me ten minutes with him," pleaded Sharie.

"No! We don't have time!" shouted Stinky.

"We gave you guys a whole day to snap out of your fake make-believe superstar status. You can at least give me a few minutes," Sharie stated, and with that, she was off with Jeffery a few feet away.

What could we say? She was right. Had it not been for Ryan and Stinky, we could have been gone a day ago by now. Although the rest of us didn't object to Sharie and Jeffery hopefully just saying their goodbyes, I was a little concerned about what he might want to say to her. I was well aware that we all needed to go back together. So, my fake friends and I stayed near them, pretending to be engrossed in our own conversation.

"This is crazy," one of the fake friends said. I couldn't tell who had said it. It was getting harder to tell them apart. They looked like me, dressed like me, and the more I was around them, the more they sounded like me. *Nah*, I quickly dismissed that idea. They couldn't take my speech. I watched Jeffery and Sharie hug. It was innocent and pure, and for a moment I wondered if they had the real thing.

"Well, I guess we won't be going to Disney World after all," Jeffery said.

"No, we won't," said Sharie. "We've got to move fast, Jeffery. I want you to know I had a nice time, and I don't blame you for anything. I now know what it is to fly."

We could tell that Jeffery was really getting choked up. Then he whispered, "I re-learned what it is to be young and curious again. I had forgotten that you see."

They laughed and the rest of us wished we were in on the joke. Jeffery reached out and held Sharie and we knew that this was very unusual. To be honest, it made me uncomfortable. Then he whispered to her, "The animals can talk, instruct the—"

Before he could finish the phrase, one of the fake friends hit him on the back of the head and he collapsed in Sharie's arms. She lowered him gently to the ground.

"What did you do that for, Sal?"

"I didn't do that," Sal protested.

"I did it," confessed Sallemae. "If he would have held you any longer, the two of you could have become one. I don't know about you, but I need you guys to get to that wall. I want to live."

"He wasn't going to do that," cried Sharie.

"But we don't know for sure," I said, "and it's better to be safe than sorry, Sharie. We've got to go!"

On that note, we were again moving toward the wall. We were so close that we could see the light reflecting on the wall. It started to rain, but that didn't stop us, even though the ground was getting muddy. Our legs were moving slower, but we kept moving.

At some point, Stinky got stuck in the mud; it appeared it was getting deeper and harder to move through. We pulled together and helped Stinky regain the strength of his legs, then kept moving. We struggled through stuff so dirty and grimy it felt like we were walking through concrete, so I shouted:

"Make the ground like sand!"

As we walked, the ground became lighter and lighter until it felt like sand under our feet. We laughed. We were actually walking on sand in the middle of a desert. It was funny—so funny, we were laughing and laughing, and we couldn't stop laughing.

We were walking on sand, the sand was getting in our shoes, and personally, it was itching the bottoms of my feet, and that was funny. "Sand in my shoes," I shouted.

Marion looked and pointed at my shoes and repeated, "Sand in her shoes!" And we all started laughing, especially the twins. They found it so funny they could barely stand up. Then, the sand began to feel harder to move through. Marion was laughing so hard that he could barely say he was stuck, but he was sinking. It was then Sharie realized that the sand had turned into quicksand and that Marion was sinking.

Nothing was funny now. Marion was going deeper and deeper into the sand. We formed a line and we pulled and pulled with all our might until he was lifted out of the sand. I managed to say, "Give us ground again," and the ground appeared, and we all lay on the ground.

It surprised me when Sal said, "We got to keep moving, guys, we got to keep moving."

We got back up and started walking again; none of us had legs that could move faster than a walk, but we were moving.

The wall looked so far away, yet it was so bright. All of a sudden, Ryan yelled out, "Watch out for the scorpions!"

The sand had left behind scorpions. I yelled. We were being stung by scorpions. We were throwing and stomping scorpions all over the place, sometimes at each other. Ryan threw one right into Sharie's hair and she almost fainted, but I got it out of her hair and back home.

This was becoming too much, but we couldn't give up. We felt a strange feeling, the stings—like little electrical jolts through our skin. "Get rid of the scorpions!" we were yelling, but soon as they disappeared, they reappeared even bigger, so we kept screaming until Stinky yelled, "Get rid of all the scorpions in the world for life!" and we didn't see anything else.

We were now in the midst of a wilderness, with grounds made of hard rock that hurt to walk on. Although we didn't see the presence of Gill, we sure felt it, and every now and again one of us would just get punched in the face.

"What was that!" yelled Marion. "You guys feel that?"

These punches were coming quick and fast, and Marion could not fight the air. Although all of us were being hit, Marion was obviously taking more blows. Soon enough, he doubled over and appeared to be spitting up blood.

I bent down and whispered in Marion's ear, "Look, we got to keep moving. We have less than four hours, get on your feet and fight!"

Marion started to fight; it was like he was hitting the air and missing, but the invisible punches weren't missing him. We yelled, "Stop fighting Marion!" and then *we* would get hit again. Ryan had a bloody nose, but he was still yelling "Stop fighting Marion!" Sharie was being dragged by the hair, and even Sal and Sallemae were getting hit.

Out of the blue, Stinky yelled: "Gill, die!"

The punching stopped, and we all managed to get back on our feet. I had been hit so hard in the chest that it felt like my heart stopped, but I got back up. We were in rough shape—cracked bones, bruises, bloody mouths and noses—but we were moving.

No one wanted to acknowledge that the light was getting dimmer and we were feeling human again. Only a few of us could speak and make things really happen. I didn't want to say anything just in case this would hurt our chances, but we really needed Ryan and Stinky. It was as if they still had the most power. So we were moving as fast as humanly possible. We wouldn't stop. We had two hours.

We met creepy reptiles on the way and commanded them to die, determined not to let them stop us. As we moved on, we heard the hissing sound of snakes and realized that it could be Gill watching us and trying to create a roadblock. Sharie hadn't totally gotten over the fact that her friend was left in the woods, and she kept repeating to herself what Jeffery had said about the animals.

We continued moving toward the wall with the light. We could hear the snakes, but we couldn't see them. It was just the sound. We came to a pond, which was surprising, for a pond was not on the map. We all knew what was in ponds, and before we could say the words, there, slowly rippling through the water, was a grayish-green alligator.

"We command you to die!" shouted Stinky.

But the alligator didn't die, it just moved back under the water.

"It didn't die!" I screamed.

"Well," said Sal lazily, "at some point, you do lose your power. We can't all speak things into being. You knew that already."

If eyes could kill, Sal would have been dead at this point. Truthfully, I think we all distrusted them, but we were literally just steps from the wall and minutes from home. So, I shouted, "Tell us now how we can defeat it, or you get fed to it!"

I guess Sal knew this wasn't what she wanted, and if she didn't come up with something fast, she would be alligator soup.

"Calm down," said Sallemae. "What's more ferocious than an alligator?"

"A tiger!" shouted Stinky.

"But a tiger won't go near a muddy alligator pond."

"A crocodile!" shouted Ryan.

"They could co-exist. What's something alligators are afraid of?"

Then it hit me—hippos! I remembered watching on an animal channel that alligators and crocodiles are deathly afraid of hippos, so we ordered four hippos to take us to the other side of the pond, and so they did. We demanded that they be faster than normal and, as we rode on the backs of these big, beastly animals, we noticed that the alligator moved away from us.

We quickly got off the hippos, for it wasn't a pleasant ride, and just as Marion was about to get off, one of the hippos chomped on his arm and started dragging him back into the lake. We commanded the hippos to disappear, but we were left with a screaming, yelling Marion with a broken arm.

"I can't feel my face, I can't feel my face!" he cried.

Stinky sat down and covered his own face, as he had never seen his brother display anything but bravery. Ryan had nearly fainted, as he had never seen that much blood in his life.

Calmly, Sharie said, "I demand Marion be whole again." Instantly Marion was whole again. He got up and rubbed his face, swinging his arm to test it. We were all crying and laughing at the same time. Sharie still had the power to speak things, and she was fast on her feet.

"Thank you, Sharie!" I shouted.

"Let's get to the wall, people," said Sal.

And we realized she was right. All we wanted to do was get out of this make-believe world from hell—the sooner the better.

With our own sense of joy and release, we all walked to the well-lit wall, and that was it. There wasn't a hole in the wall like there had been before. It was just a well-lit wall. We bumped the wall and tried to move it back. But it wasn't the wall. We had traveled for hours just to discover this wasn't the right wall. We were exasperated. My pretend friends were crying, yelling, and screaming as if they were about to die.

"Shut up!" I ordered them.

They were used to this place, we weren't. They had made a decision to stay past the five days, we hadn't. We wanted out—I wasn't about to put up with their overreactions and shenanigans.

"I say we kill them!" Marion shouted.

"Then we will be murderers," Sharie protested. Her grandmother had always taught her not to kill, not even with words.

Ryan was in recovery mode. He looked at the map again, this time with more clarity. "I say we go to this location. It is on the other side, but we could go underground this time."

"No!" shouted Sal. "You don't want to do that!"

"I say we go underground. What do you say, Ryan? The last thing we want to do is listen to them," I said.

Sharie looked at the now-darkening sky and asked for a raven to appear, and out of nowhere, it appeared.

"I thought we couldn't speak things anymore," shouted Marion.

"Stop yelling at me." I redirected Marion's anger to the two hugging girls.

"Oh," he said, then he shouted at them, "I thought we couldn't speak things?"

Sallemae stood right in front of Marion's face as if she was there to tell him they were not afraid. They looked at Sharie who was now bending over, and we all knew speaking those words had almost knocked the wind out of her. We felt it too. The more we spoke, the weaker we became, but Marion was still looking to the girls for answers.

"I said you wouldn't be able to speak *everything*, and trust me, you won't, as you will very soon find out. The more you become a part of this world, the less effective your power will be. In about two hours, you will be just like us, or rather, like we used to be. I'm also tired of the distrust. If we could just leave to deceive the next innocent fools, then why would we stay with you? It's not like I enjoy being around you guys either, for the record. However, we've got to see you to the wall, or we — and you — will be stuck in a situation you will wish to be out of for most nights to come. You think we don't want to exist, just because we can't exist in the other world anymore? Well, think again! We are here — go ahead, Salle, just try wishing us away, 'cause honey, that would be useless."

"Go away now!" I shouted.

Sal and Sallemae just stood there with arms folded, not moving at all.

"Again, we're in this together, and going underground is foolish."

I could see that Sharie was now enjoying the raven resting on her shoulder.

"I didn't think you liked birds so much," I said.

"Well, usually I don't, but I remember Jeffery telling me something about how the animals can talk ..." Sharie turned to the raven. "How can we get back home? Please tell me."

"Well ..." began the bird—and if you could see our expressions at that moment, you would think we had just seen a ghost—"they are right about one thing: underground is dangerous."

"See, we told you," said Sallemae.

"There is another wall around the mountain. Let me see the map," instructed the raven.

Ryan opened the map and the raven used his claw to point the way through the mountain for us to get to an open wall.

"Will there be much danger there?" Sharie asked.

"Well, there are mountain lions and wolves, but if you meet them, simply ask for a larger animal to take them down, and don't stick

236

around to watch the fight. You must keep moving."

"Can we make it there in two hours?" asked Ryan.

"You can. I will lead you as far as I'm able. Gill is after you guys, isn't he?"

We all nodded yes.

"He will for sure have me killed by lightning or something. When I fly back up, ask one thousand birds to show you the way, then I will be just one in a thousand. He can't kill us all in two hours, but if he does manage to kill us all somehow, just remember you've got the road map. Look at it closely, make sure it's in your heart as well as on paper."

The raven flew back up to the sky and we *commanded* that one thousand birds show us the way. And when we looked up, we saw a sky full of white ravens leading the way.

"How did you know to do that?" I asked Sharie. I knew that animals were living here. I had been inside Gill's house. But I didn't know we could ask them for help and that they could speak like human beings.

Sharie answered with a little pride in her voice, "Jeffery was a real true friend — about as real as this world could offer, I guess."

I guess she could have been right about Jeffery. But as for the two working with us now, *that* I wouldn't bank on.

21

INTO THE MOUNTAINS

Reddish-brown dust covered our clothes and shoes as we plodded through the mountain terrain. We were glad Sharie did mountain climbing; she was able to speak things we'd never heard of that she knew we would need. I also noticed that when she spoke, we didn't get everything. The dog never appeared. I didn't know about the rest of them, but I was feeling odd. Before, I'd felt light. Now, I was feeling like I'd just eaten a seven-course meal. I wondered if everyone felt full.

When it was decided that we would be taking the mountains, I pictured a big hilly spread, made up mostly of rocks, and us holding on to ropes and sticks as we conducted the sport of mountaineering. However, it wasn't like that. We were simply following a well-plowed red dirt path. Occasionally, we would see a few people, almost in silhouette, sort of floating by us, making sure not to give eye contact.

I worried for a moment that one could be Gill in disguise. I wasn't sure, since I'd never seen his face, but in my mind, Gill could be almost anything and anybody. You had to see that image in order to believe it. So, when we saw the figures of people, we all tried to get a little closer, as if we were just checking out the surroundings.

Learned Kansan was a place where people were planted through no choice of their own. They had roles to fill and duties to perform. As long as they were happy with who they'd decided to be, I guess they could live a peaceful existence. But I didn't want to live my life marked as just one type of person with only one role to fill. I wanted the flexibility of being able to do what I wanted, to be what I wanted to be, and to grow. With that in mind, I picked up the pace a little.

"You can see a glowing light from here, can't you?" Stinky shouted.

We all nodded at Stinky. At that moment, he seemed so much older than eight, but he was really just a kid. We were all just kids, really. The oldest one in the group was Marion and he was only thirteen and a half. The rest of us were just twelve or barely thirteen.

The half-point birthday was Marion's idea. He was the only one who got to claim it because he was at least four months older than all of us. Deep down, I believed this was just his way of getting two gifts for his birthday. However, we didn't mind giving extra to Marion. He gave to us most of the year. If we were short on cash or on a Link card, he always filled in the gap and helped out. I guess that came from being a little older, and I suppose that was worth celebrating.

I looked up at the skies and noticed there were fewer birds, but they were still leading the way.

For some reason, Stinky felt like confessing, so he started talking. "When I get home, I'm going to tell my mom, 'No more being bad.' I'm going to do what I am told. No more exploring, no more talking back to adults, and no more stealing from the store or fighting. That's right, you heard me; I am not going to steal anymore. I'm simply goin' to children's church and I'll eat when they serve hot dogs.

"And no more music — turns out the life of a rock star doesn't really rock at all. This is all I am gon' do — go home, watch television, eat dinner, give my mom a kiss at night, sometimes write my dad a letter, wake up on time, go to school on time, and do my homework. If we have to spend the whole summer in detention, I won't cry or complain! I'm just gon' do it, just like that. I'm just gon' sit there and keep my big mouth shut. People be sayin' I talk too much and maybe they're right. Maybe everyone's been right all along. Maybe ... maybe I am just a bad little shorty."

"Stop beating yourself up," said Ryan. "We all could do a little better. When I get home, I'm going to tell my mother how much I love her and that I won't be needing to see my biological dad anymore, even if he does want to see me. I'm going to make sure I tell her that I love her because I do, man; I love my mom!"

Then Ryan started to cry and it was real, not fake. It was real and touching — so touching that Stinky started crying too, and now we had two boys crying on the side of the rocky mountain.

"Enough!" said Sal. "We've got to move it!"

"Cool it, Salle. Everyone can take a moment," said Sharie, "but we do have to keep moving, boys."

"I didn't say that, Sharie. It was one of the fake friends. But I'm with you. We got to move it."

I didn't argue with Sharie because honestly, as much as I wanted to move on, in my heart, I think I understood why Stinky and Ryan were experiencing their little meltdown. I was feeling it too. I was thinking that if we had just gone straight home instead of taking the long way home to avoid punishment, we would have missed the wall altogether. Instead, we were here in Learned Kansan, watching the sky darken and the birds decrease as we felt our way along rocks we could not see while an eerie light appeared on the horizon.

As the sky got darker and the light brightened, a host of nocturnal animals peered behind small bushes to watch us. We continued on, determined. A family of raccoons came out and chattered at us. It felt strange, as if we were running a marathon and the raccoons, squirrels, and geckos were our sideline cheerleaders. We didn't stop moving, nor did we bask in the glory of the whistling and cheers; we just moved as fast as our feet would allow. Our eyes were on the prize, and we were going for it!

A short distance ahead of us, we saw a shadow — one so large and black that it shaded one-third of the light behind the rock we were headed toward.

"I was afraid of this," whispered Sal.

We didn't respond but kept a steady pace toward the figure. It wasn't going to surprise us, now that we'd seen it already, but we were pretty sure it would frighten us. Still, we moved forward.

22

THE BEAST BEHIND THE SHADOW

It was not long before we were face to face with a ten-foot-tall, 1,200-pound Kodiak bear. He was sitting at ease, waiting on us.

"So, tell us, Sal ... Sallemae ... what should we do now?"

They looked genuinely surprised, and neither said a word.

The huge, oversized bear stood up and growled, "I wondered what took you all so long!"

"Go away right now, you big stupid bear!" said Stinky

The bear did not move, but we all took three steps back. We looked to the left and to the right of us—there was nothing but a downward fall. It hadn't felt like we were going around and around a mountain, but now we knew that was exactly what we had been doing. The bear would not be moved — at least, not by our words or apparent display of bravery — so Marion tried another approach.

"Look, big talking bear dude, we would love to stay and chat, but truthfully, we got a wall to get to, so whatever it is you want, just say it, OK?"

The bear's words came out slow and intentional. "Well, well, young man, since you asked nicely, I will try and be as brief as possible. I simply want your lives. Not much, just all of your heads."

The bear stomped his feet and the earth shook. We huddled together in terror — if we were going to die, it would be together. Then I thought, *Wait a minute, we are NOT going to die. We've got to fight.*

So, I said, "Well, Mr. Scary Bear, our lives are something we're not prepared to give up without a fight, so ... let's do this!"

In an instant, we were all armed with bats, guns, ball-and-chains, and knives. We all called out weapons we were pretty sure we could handle well.

"Calm down, my little chickpeas. Surely, we are going to fight, but not with everyone," said the bear.

"Oh, yeah?" yelled Marion, "then who do you want to fight?"

"It's not so much who I want to fight," answered the bear, "but there are rules in the mountains. It's who I have to fight."

"And who is that?" asked Marion.

"The first person who spoke to me is my most worthy opponent."

We all hugged Marion to assure him that we were in his corner.

"I guess if you got to fight me, then let's go," said Marion bravely.

"But, but … you weren't the first person to say something to me," protested the bear, "I believe it was —"

He didn't even have to say the name, for the hairy brown bear with his long claws and beady eyes was looking straight at Stinky. We all turned to see what he would do.

"You fat pig, I ain't fighting you!"

"I'm insulted. Do I look like a pig to you? Trust me, I can carry my weight."

"Hey who's making these rules?" asked Marion. "Why can't you fight me, I'm still much smaller than you."

"These are the rules of the mountain, didn't you read them?"

"We were never given any rules, so I think you're lying!" said Marion.

"Am I lying about the fact that your little brother has a big mouth and is always getting in trouble in that city … what's the name of the city? '*Chicago*.' You didn't call for the rules, and I guess that's why you didn't read them. That's OK, but if you guys kill me, which I don't think will happen, you all will stay here and never get back to that big city you long for." The bear stood on two legs and sharpened his paws with a large rock.

"I can't fight!" Stinky panicked. "I can't! I can't!"

The bear was getting a little too much pleasure out of seeing Stinky cry and lie down on the ground, kicking his little legs. We decided that we needed a time-out. Sharie took one arm, I took the other arm, Ryan took a leg, Marion took the other leg, and we moved Stinky back about ten steps from the bear. We needed a little one-on-one time with him.

One thing we knew about Stinky was that if you put him in a corner, he would come out swinging. We needed the fight in him to come alive. Marion had a way of handling Stinky; he was more than just his big brother, he was like a substitute father, so when he whispered to Stinky, Stinky listened.

"Stinky, this bear could be just one big liar, or he could be telling the truth, which means you are our only hope, and if I had only one person in this world to count on I would rather it be you. I need you to calm down and listen. Now, when have you known me to put you in a battle that I wouldn't fight for you?"

"I can't do it. I can't!"

"That's exactly what he's counting on, and so is Gill and all the rest. If you don't fight, then we stay stuck here in this place. We'll only be a dream for other people, when and if they ever call on a couple of has-been rappers. Look, all I want you to do is—"

Marion pulled Stinky off to the side and finished instructing him, just in case the mini-mes were traitors—there were still elements of distrust in the camp. We didn't know what he said to Stinky, but we could see that the little boy was ready to fight the bear. If he was afraid, we could no longer see it. The bear was now circling around, showing off his two advantages—he could fight on all fours or standing on two legs.

"If the kid's ready, I'm hungry," taunted the bear.

"Oh, I'm ready alright!" bragged Stinky.

The bear sharpened his already long, sharp claws on a big rock to the side of him. As he scraped his claws up and down on the rock, we could see his claw marks in the stone. Then he threw the massive rock and ran toward Stinky. Stinky commanded two weapons, a rock and a long spear.

The bear stood on two feet, and his ten-foot height was now even more obvious. We were all yelling to Stinky, "That's a scare tactic, don't fall for it, giants fall faster!"

The bear stood just a little lower to the ground before he came at Stinky. And come at Stinky he did! In sort of a skipping motion he ran toward Stinky, bringing the mountainside with him as rocks started to fall from the side and behind him. For a moment, we thought we all would roll under the rocks or be hit by one of them. Stinky rolled between the bear's legs and the bear stomped angrily, shaking the ground, but thankfully missing Stinky.

This time, the bear was making shrill, high-pitched sounds, sort of cooing at Stinky. We knew that Stinky going between his legs had really angered the bear. We could see the bear wanted this to end. The bear got on all four legs and ran toward Stinky, who was now hiding behind the rock. The bear stood and begin to walk on two legs with open claws ready to rip Stinky to pieces.

He charged at the rock. Stinky moved quickly and threw a stone at the bear's spine, which hit his high shoulders. You could tell this hurt, but he was still moving toward Stinky. The bear was using all of his advantages to scare Stinky, and Stinky was using his advantages—his abilities to hide in small spaces behind rocks and move quickly.

At one point, the bear tossed a boulder at Stinky; meanwhile, Stinky was hitting the bear with smaller but equally hard rocks. He hit the bear's baby toe, which made the bear move at a slower pace. Then, with all the force a kid could muster up, Stinky threw another rock right at the center of the bear's face, and it did not miss. Little did the bear know Stinky was a pitcher, and he could throw really hard and fast.

The bear stumbled back just a little, but he was still moving toward Stinky, so with all his might, Stinky took his spear and thrust it into the bear's stomach. The bear moved back and stood up, and you could see the blood dripping from the center. With a spear in his stomach, the bear still did not want to give up. He was angry and very hurt, even dizzy, but he was still moving toward Stinky as if he just needed to get one good whack at him—but Stinky was too fast.

The bear was wobbling from side to side but still trying to catch Stinky. We were yelling and cheering, "Go, Stinky! You killing him, you killing him!" The bear turned to look at us as if he was going to break the rules and charge at us, and we all thought this would be his next move, but instead, he slipped on a rock and toppled off the mountain.

We all looked and cheered as we watched the bear fall ungracefully, paws right out to the sides as he was flying to his well-deserved death. And there stood Stinky, still not sure he was alive; we started picking him up and patting him on the head and back.

Stinky grabbed his spear, turned around quickly without looking, and the spear went straight through Ryan's stomach. All we could hear was Ryan mumble, "You did good, Stinky," before he fell to the ground.

The moment went from celebration to devastation. We all ran to Ryan. He was unable to speak, but we could see he wanted to say something. A small tear was forming in the corner of his eyes that slowly released as we watched him try and catch his breath.

"Ryan, don't do this!" I shouted. "Don't die!"

Ryan was trying to fight it. Marion tore off his jacket and plugged his hole to slow down the bleeding. Sharie and I were yelling, "Ryan, be whole!" We had done that before and it had worked, so we were now hysterically screaming, "Ryan, be whole!"

I yelled, "Don't close your eyes, don't!" I watched as green eyes turned to darker green, and my one last prayer was that his eyes would not turn black. "Don't you dare die," I commanded, and as though it was fate, he had a heartbeat.

Sharie had things in her mountain bag that we used. We poured alcohol on the wound and some form of white cream, and we patched the hole. It had totally soaked Marion's shirt with blood, but plugging it with the cotton patching appeared to have helped out a little. He was still breathing.

We all noticed that Sallemae and Sal were standing off to the side, just looking, not really concerned. They didn't show any emotion, as was as if they were simply waiting for something and looking at their watches. It also looked as if Sallemae was trying to tell Sal something, but there was an air of superiority that was emerging from this girl in our group. We all heard an alarm go off and we instantly looked at Sallemae. She stood up and walked to the middle of the circle in full confidence about what she wanted to say to us.

"Go ahead, let him die," she announced. "It's over because your time is up. In exactly five minutes, Gill is going to come down and pronounce your new assignment."

"No, Ryan!" I cried. "Grab his legs and arm. We got five minutes; we can do it."

We were sweating and panicking as we all grabbed body parts.

"Look," Sallemae said again, "it's no use. Besides, those birds are not exactly the smartest of flying animals. Why didn't you call on an eagle? Really, you're something like twenty minutes away from the wall. We passed it coming up."

"How could you?" I shouted. "How could you let us get stuck here?"

"Don't you dare spoil, little girl. Good people don't come here, so shut up and suck it up. You will learn to like it or you won't."

"I hate you!" I shouted.

And Sharie shouted right behind me, "Go to hell!"

"Look, girl," said Sallemae, "I been living in hell a long time. It's time for you guys to visit that place."

Sallemae laughed a witch's laugh, and her true self was slowly coming through her skin.

"What's taking Gill so long?" Sallemae said.

You could see that Sal was not happy, as it appeared that Gill was not coming down to claim his prize. It also appeared that something was messed up with Sallemae's assessment of this situation.

"You fool!" yelled Sal, "Always think you know it all. I wanted to go home, too. It was never going to happen this time. Salle with an 'E' gave us a run for our money for sure, but *you* made us lose. Where's Gill? You always think you're so smart, that you know everything."

"Well, three families are here for life because of me, so what the heck, I'm not that bad," said Sallemae.

"Wait a minute," I said. "You are from New York, I remember that, and we are from Chicago. You are an hour ahead of us. Gill ain't coming because we can't lose for another hour. Let's go!"

Sallemae looked as if someone had just snatched the life out of her body.

"You always think you know so much. How did you plan to replace Salle or Sharie when you don't speak sign language? Won't matter anyhow. Now I can't get back home because of your big mouth," said Sal angrily.

"What the hell you talking about?" said Sallemae.

Sal grabbed Sallemae by the neck and threw her to the ground. Sallemae got back up and started hitting her in the face. They were kicking and pulling hair. Sal tripped Sallemae on the ground and kicked her off the mountain. The last image of Sallemae we saw was her falling backward from the mountain. We all ran to the edge to see if she landed, and she did. We turned our heads. We were sure it was too far down to see the blood spatter, but just seeing her fall, we could imagine it.

You could see in Sal's eyes that this wasn't what she preferred, but something bigger was at stake. She also knew that Sallemae could not complete this task, for us kids were a little too smart for that. Sal pulled herself together, wiped her eyes, and with all the sincerity she could muster up, she said, "Now, I know you guys have no reason to trust me, but I can take you where you need to go in time."

"I don't trust her," I said. "But we've got to get home, and we have around forty-five minutes to get there."

"Look, Salle, I've got to go home. Sallemae hated her life in New York, but I didn't hate my life. I was a bank teller. I just want my life back."

We looked at Sal. She had to just get home, and really, that's all any of us wanted to do. Just go home. Then, Sal said something that we all wanted to hear.

"The closer to the wall Ryan gets, the better he will become."

We all jumped up. We had to get him to the wall and back home—he was going back with us even if he had to go in pieces! Marion picked up his upper body, Sharie carried a leg, and I was about to pick up his other leg when I saw Stinky sitting with his head bowed on the side of the rock.

I put down Ryan's leg and went and sat next to Stinky. I knew we were under the gun, but we needed Stinky, and we needed him ready to fight. I looked at Stinky, who had just defeated a ten-foot bear, sitting with his head bowed. I guess it was still hard for him to believe his friend was lying there, barely breathing, and he was to blame.

I walked over to Stinky and said, "Look, Stinky, Ryan was family to us all. He was the one who made us laugh when we really wanted to cry. He made adventures out of chasing rats and magical music out of garbage can tops. He wouldn't give up on us, so we can't give up on him."

"But I killed him," said Stinky.

"Stinky, that's not your fault; no one here blames you. We know that you would take a bullet for Ryan if you had to; but most importantly, Ryan knows this as well. Let's get him back home so that he can complain about you making his bed smell, and you can complain about him cheating in games, and both of you guys can complain about the fact that I think I am always right—which I am, but that's another story."

I could see that this was sinking in, but it wasn't yet moving him to move, and we didn't have much time.

"Look, kid," I said as if I had suddenly become an adult. "You accidentally almost killed him, but he ain't dead yet, and that wasn't your fault. You got a lot of fight in you kid, a whole lot of fight in you."

I whispered something to him that my grandfather told me, and I'd never really shared this with anyone. "Out of all the things my grandpa says to me, there's one thing that actually makes sense. He says fighters never stop fighting in life, they just find new battles to fight. This, Stinky, is just another battle we got to fight."

With that, Stinky jumped up, picked that spear up off the ground, threw it over the mountain, and went and helped Marion carry Ryan.

We all followed Sal, hoping that she wanted home as much as we did, and from the sight of it, it sure did look that way. She was moving as fast as we asked her to; we all had one thing on our minds, and it wasn't the fact that our feet hurt, or our hands had blood on them, or our hair had sweated into pure hard knots, or dirt mixed with sweat was crawling down the sides of our faces — none of that mattered.

The only thing that mattered at this point was that we all got to the wall together. That was where we were headed toward … *the wall!*

23

THE WALL

Tenaciously, we carried Ryan up a narrow path that gave way to a small ravine with streams of water trickling down it. We saw a small wooden shack that looked familiar. It had a wire gate with a few sheep in the yard. I found myself looking ahead at the light and then wondering if we should head to the shack instead. The light was so bright. The wall was still lit, and it looked like a place we should visit, but I didn't know why.

"Hey, y'all, you want to stop at the shack?" I managed to ask, out of breath. "I sure am dehydrated!"

"No!" shouted Sal. "Everything here is a distraction."

"What's the matter with you?" they questioned me.

I was thinking that we were not that far away, but in fact, I didn't know why I said that. What was I thinking? Were my thoughts not my own? It was as if someone was telling me to say things, or as if the words came out of my mouth and that as they were exiting, I knew they were not my words. Were my thoughts even my own? *Think.*

"Yeah!" Marion looked at me fearlessly. "What's the matter with you?"

"Well, *ex-cuuuuse* me for *living!*" I said. But I really didn't want to say that. Really, I didn't. Thoughts were running hurdles through my mind; it's like I didn't know which one to actually pick and choose from, I was so tired.

I was slightly hurt that Marion had given me that look—what was that all about? We had been friends, each other's protectors, and then I got that look? I only wanted a bath and a drink of water, not a fight. My legs were cramping up. Sal was now holding onto my arm as if to drag me along. No one noticed that Sal had pushed my arm off Ryan and she was now helping Ryan. I was going to say something, but I was tired, really tired, and didn't want to stop for conversation.

What had I done to them that they didn't even care that my arms were scraped up and bleeding? I got a second wind, broke away from them, and walked my tired, aching legs over to Sharie to see if she would care. She just looked at me as if I was irritating her; but I was a mess—covered in dirt, bloody.

It didn't matter. "We only have fifteen minutes left," I said, and so I moved on as I found myself leading the way and knowing exactly what way to go.

The sky was now totally dark and there were only three birds remaining above us. We hadn't known that most of the birds had been just following the leader, and when Gill finally killed the bird that saw the map, the rest had simply kept going. Had we known better, we would have let several hundred birds look at the map.

Suddenly, it started to rain. It was pouring so hard we could barely see the wall. We looked up and the birds were all gone. Big eagles, the size of six-foot-tall men, were throwing balls of lightning at us. They felt like electric shocks when they hit us.

"What are they doing?" Marion yelled.

"What do they look like they are doing?" I yelled back. "They're trying to kill us!"

The rain and balls of lightning were coming at us so furiously and fast-paced that we had to skip and jump as if we were playing dodgeball to get to the wall. I saw a few lightning balls hit Ryan and he moved just a little. This gave me hope. Sal was right, he was coming back to life, so the way was near. We came to a fork in the road—we didn't know which way to take. "Where are those birds when we really need them?" I asked.

Ryan was moaning that he wanted to stand up. We hugged him, but all he could do was moan.

"Take out the map," suggested Sharie.

It was the way she said, "Take out the map." It almost sounded muffled, twisted. We only heard the *ake* in take and the *ap* in map. Sharie was holding her ears, but what she wasn't telling us was that the closer we got to the wall, the more distant her hearing—and her voice— became. Words that had been flowing flawlessly were harder to come by.

I took the map from my pocket and showed it to Ryan, who was still having trouble breathing, but was conscious. We had a choice to make, and only fourteen minutes to make it before becoming permanent fixtures in Learned Kansan, bound to a future we didn't want nor knew much about.

"... et ... o ... is ... ay!" Sharie was trying to tell us something.

We thought she said, "Let's go this way," but we weren't sure. We let her lead the way. With only thirteen minutes left, we skipped, ducked, and rolled our way down the path Sharie chose, and lucky for us, it was the right one! We'd made it!

As we were celebrating, hugging and crying because we'd made it with fifteen minutes to spare, but just when we were about to move to the portal, Gill emerged out of the wall. He wasn't the clean, nice-looking guide we'd seen the first day. His face looked like gray dirt, and his hair was covered in a black wrapping, but clearly, something was living and moving underneath that wrap. He walked toward us and we all couldn't help but move back.

"I know you didn't think it would be that easy," he said, blowing dirt in our faces and covering our eyes.

"You can't stop us now, Gill. We beat you. We found the wall," said Sal, and I was sure she was trying to take over my identity. She was saying what I wanted to say, and then she shouted what I wanted to say next: "So, go away!"

Before I could say something, Gill blew, and Sal was raised five feet off the ground and dropped to the floor. We all stared at Gill.

"Kids, I have to admit you're much smarter than your adult counterparts," he said, "but that won't change how this ends."

"We've got to get out of here," Marion said. "My mother's counting on me. "

"I don't care," said Gill. "My world is counting on me. Besides, how will we one day have a society if we just let people get away with killing each other? There is a murderer among you. We have a better world coming and for the few of you mortals who will get to see this world, you must learn to play fair. How can I let you get away with murder? Someone has to be punished."

"It's her," I said, "lying on the floor."

Although Sal couldn't say much, she pointed at me. And I saw, with my own eyes, Marion went over and helped Sal up. Was he really buying this? No, I knew he knew better!

"I got to pee," said Stinky. "Man, do I gotta go."

"The only place you are going is to sleep in my laboratory. "

"Hey, but I don't wanna go there! I said I got to pee."

Gill threw back his head and focused his eyes on Stinky. They were red and scary, and Stinky stood straight as if he no longer had to pee.

Gill watched Stinky not being able to move with pleasure. Then he said, jokingly, "Just pee on yourself, one would think you would be used to that by now."

One thing I know about Stinky is that he doesn't like you talking about his smell. I am sure he knew he smelled—that was why we called him Stinky—but he didn't like you to say he smelled. He couldn't move his body, and his arms looked as if they were glued to his sides, but he opened his mouth and started singing as loud as he possibly could sing in a key so high it pierced our hearing: "You can ring my bell in the morning, bell, bell, you can ring my bell at night, bell, but don't ring my bell if you ain't got no money to pay my bills! Ring my bell like rain failing from sky, bells ring like midnight at night …"

Strangely, this caused Gill to move back. I think it was something about the sound of bells he couldn't take. I thought back, and I couldn't find an example of bells anywhere in Learned Kansan. Gill was moving back quickly—this was a sound he couldn't live with—so all we could think of was to say the word "bells."

I whispered in Ryan's ear, "Sing, please sing."

I heard him say one word, "Bells," and like thunder, it started to rain bells.

267

As the bells rang, we all started to sing the song, and I cried out for bell sounds as Gill was slowly moving backward from us. I just knew it wasn't the song, but rather the sound of the bells that he couldn't take. So, I—not Sal—kept crying out for bells and cymbals.

As Gill merged back into the rock, he was moving further and further away from us and getting smaller. Soon, we didn't see him anymore, but we could still feel the pressure in our heads like we were going to blow our tops and our heads were going to explode. As he was moving back, he was throwing everything attached to his body at us. We had to throw off snakes that were slowly crawling up our legs and arms and wrapping around our ankles. The flies were so thick they were covering our eyes and our noses. We felt the slimy feel of frogs that were hopping all around the place, but we continued to sing until the portal was visible again; I could no longer feel the pressure in my head, and I looked over at Sharie and knew she must be feeling better, too. My legs felt like rubble, my muscles hurt, and my hands felt like every finger was broken, but we smiled at each other because we could see the portal. Gill was leaving, and the portal became brighter and brighter.

We still had time to leave, and leave we were going to, covered in dirt, frog slime, and bug juice. We were going to leave this place—with fewer limbs if we had to.

But there was one more dragon to slay, and she was really playing me. If I had an academy award to give, she would win.

"Yeah, goodbye, Gill see you never," said Sal as she grabbed Ryan's hand.

"What are you doing?" I demanded. "You're not going back, Sal, I am!"

"What? You are not going back, Sal, *I* am the one going back."

"Wait a minute, did you just call me Sal? Are you kidding me?" I asked in disbelief. "I'm Salle with an 'E,'" I corrected.

"No, I'm Salle with an 'E,'" said Sal.

Sharie, Stinky, Ryan, and Marion just looked at the two identical Salles with an 'E' standing in front of them.

"Will the real Salle with an 'E' from the West Side of Chicago please stand?" said Marion.

"I'm already standing!" Sal and I said at the same time. I felt a wave of anger like never before take over my body, and with all of my might, I knocked Sal to the ground, where she stayed.

"Now we have one," Stinky said.

But Sal got back up, looking exactly like me, with blood and mud in the exact same places, and I couldn't help but wonder: *When did that happen?*

I looked at Sal and she looked at me. Oh yeah, she and I were both ready, but that wouldn't solve the problem facing us. Only one of us could go. I had to make sure it was me.

24

SALLE WHO?

The two of us stood there at the wall. I was so angry that I began slapping that phony, and she slapped me back. For a while, you would have thought we were auditioning for a Three Stooges comeback show.

"Wait a minute," said Ryan, "I know how we can do this — how many family members do you have?"

"Three," we both answered.

"That didn't turn out so well," Ryan said.

"Look, let's just go; hold my hand," I said. I reached out to Marion, but he wouldn't touch me. In fact, I was pretty sure he thought Sal was really me.

"I don't know for sure which one is Salle," he said, "but I do know for sure it's not her." He pointed at me, the real Salle.

"Are you crazy, Marion?" I argued. "I am me, Salle, with an 'E.' I know I look like a mess, but I'm the one who figured this place out from the start. Look, if … if you can't choose the real Salle, *WHICH IS ME*, then we're all gonna be stuck in this world forever. That's what they've wanted all along. They spent the last two days learning all about this moment just so they could trick you!"

"She's crazy. Remember, Marion, how I was telling you how I missed my family and my way of life? She wasn't here with us, so she couldn't know we had that conversation," Sal lied.

"It's her," Marion said, pointing to Sal, "Let's go."

"No, no, please, it's not her!" I pleaded. "She can think my thoughts now; we have merged. As soon as time runs out, you are going to see she's not me. I'm me! Stinky—I'm me!"

This was an unexpected twist that I hated for my friends to endure. If they picked the wrong one of us, we would all be stuck in this place forever. Gill would get his way, and that phony girl would get what she wanted.

"Didn't she say that they had to see us go, that we needed to go so they can live?" I reminded them. "It was probably all a lie! They probably need us to stay so they can leave."

"What I keep saying is that she's simply trying to be me," interrupted Sal. "I am really Salle, your best friend since fourth grade."

"Well, there you have it, we've been best friends since the second grade!" I said *victoriously*. Now they knew that I was in the running. It couldn't be Sal.

"I said second grade," Sal lied.

"No, she said fourth, when it was actually second. It's me, trust me," I said. "*You* are the one trying to keep us here. You lied. She lied. They set this all up. Please, someone, believe me! I am the real Salle with an 'E.' I don't want all of us to be stuck in this world. It's like a double-edged sword. You've got to pick me or they win."

"What is the name you used to call me when we were little?" asked Ryan.

Surprisingly, both of us shouted at the same time, "The Red Bomber!"

It was at this point I realized my mother was right—don't tell everybody everything you know. *What a fine time to be remembering that.* I was racking my brain for examples to prove I was me—anything—and drawing a complete blank. Then Sal took my example right out of my head.

She said, "Remember the cat we had as *children*? When we wanted to raise money for food, we would tell total strangers that if we didn't get cat food, our grandmother was going to make us give the cat away."

"That's got to be her," Marion said, pointing again at Sal, and my heart was slowly breaking.

"I told her that story, can't you see? You don't know me? Really, not any of you guys?"

Ryan shouted, "Four, we've only got four minutes!"

"Hey, I got it!" Stinky exclaimed. "Talk to her in sign language. The one who answers back is the real Salle."

And so Sharie signed, "What is your birthday?" and I signed back, "April tenth." Out of all the things I had shared with them, I never remember telling them that, and I never taught them to use sign language. I was fluent in sign language. With just three minutes left, Sharie grabbed me and we hugged like we hadn't seen each other in years. Stinky grabbed Ryan's hand, Ryan grabbed Marion, and we went into the wall, taking a very slow and deep fall.

I couldn't help but look back at Sal. The smirk on her face, the longing in her eyes; it wasn't an "Oh no, we're going to die" smirk, or an "I wish I had killed you" smirk, but rather, a "You did it, you beat us" smirk. It almost looked like Sal waved goodbye to me, but I couldn't be sure. I was simply falling to safety and enjoying the ride.

25

HOME

The sun was shining on my face. Yes, it felt like the heat of the real sun, not radiation heat, which is often how I thought the sun in Learned Kansan felt. I looked around, reaching out to feel the things my eyes laid on—my covers, my nightgown. I jumped to my feet and then felt my head. Yes! I was home, my French braids were still messed up. My mother was calling my name. *My mother!* I ran into the kitchen to find her waiting at the kitchen sink to wash my hair.

"What did I tell you to do, Salle?"

"Are you talking to me?" I asked.

"No, I'm talking to the girl standing next to you that looks just like you," my mother answered, sarcastically.

I looked around, confused, wondering if by chance she was seeing Sal or Sallemae. I looked behind me and under the table.

"What is the matter with you, Salle?" my mother asked.

"Me?" I replied.

"Yeah, you. Who else is standing in this room but you and me? Now, haven't I told you about messing up your hair after I just got it braided? That cost twenty-five dollars. Do you think your father has twenty-five dollars to throw away?"

"I guess not, but it was—"

"I already know what you are going to say, I heard it last night," my mother interrupted. "'It was Stinky and Ryan who did the experiment.' But you could've stopped Stinky and Ryan before they started that mess. You all must have known it wasn't right, now, didn't you?"

"I guess?" I admitted, making it sound more like a question.

"What if we lived in a world where people just did whatever they wanted to do and became whatever they wanted to become without effort, without rules? Would you want to live in that world?"

"Trust me, no. No, I absolutely wouldn't," I assured her.

"What is the matter with you? Are you Salle?"

"Yes!" I hugged her. In fact, I had been wanting to hug her for a long time, but with her fussing at me and all, it just hadn't seemed right. I hugged her again.

"OK, OK, so I know you get it. Rules and laws are made for a reason. We just can't go around doing whatever we want to do just because it sounds like a good idea. We've got to think, pray, reflect on the matter—and for the love of common sense, when you are not sure, ask an adult!"

"Got it! Can you sign my form? My form— you got my form, right?"

"I got your challenge slip, it's on the piano. Your father and I have decided we are not going to sign it at this time. We don't need any help, so as soon as I take down these messy, smelly braids, you can meet up with your little band of misfits and go do something good for people. Or stay in summer detention. Just means we won't be going to Key Lime Cove Water Park this summer for vacation."

She looked at me, knowing that in my mind I was thinking now of desperate measures. Why wouldn't we go, when we only spend three days there on vacation anyway? They could simply take us on a Saturday morning instead of a Friday night. That busted-down water park was the coolest thing my parents did for us, and it was the only vacation they ever took us on. How could they take that away? I looked at her, wanting to say all those things, but I also wanted to be good for some reason.

I didn't say anything except, "OK."

"OK? Who *are* you?" my mother said, looking at me like she didn't recognize me before she pushed my head under water that was much too cold. Boy, it felt good to be back home! My mind wandered to Stinky, Sharie, Marion, and Ryan. I couldn't wait to get to them to see how glad they were to be back in Chicago.

"Hurry up, Mom," I said under the water.

"You make *me* hurry up?" she replied. "You know, you have some nerve. I wouldn't have had to do this if it wasn't for ... let me think ... *you!*" she shouted.

And with much more force than I thought she needed, she loaded me down with shampoo and got to the dirty business of scrubbing my head. The water was mostly cold, as it is on a typical Saturday morning when Ryan's mother is doing laundry in the basement. However, that didn't stop my mother from getting all the soap out and applying the conditioner. I wanted to tell her, "Give me a break, I just defeated a whole world to get back to you!" But nah, I was pretty sure she wouldn't believe it.

I knew I'd better just let her put those big, one-sided braids on my head and try very hard to pretend that I liked them, for it would be a while before she paid to get my hair braided again. I could hear two sets of footsteps coming up the stairs. It was most likely Dad and Jr., and I didn't mind seeing them. I longed to see them, for it proved I was really back—back in Chicago, back with my family. *I'm back.*

26

THE CHALLENGE

When hair gets washed in the summertime, there is no blow-drying. My mother simply gives me five big braids, drowns my hair in pink lotion and carrot oil, and sends me on my way. With the oil crawling down the front and side of my face, giving me a greasy outline, I sat on the porch, not complaining and not wishing this fate away.

Any other time of year, I wouldn't come out with my hair like this. I would sit in the house until she would blow dry or straighten my hair with flat irons before I walked out of the house. However, summer was different, and today I needed to clear my head.

The more I sat with my emotions, thinking about the last couple of days, memories of Learned Kansan flip-flopping in my mind one episode after another, the more I was slowly but surely coming to think that it was all just a dream. It was vivid and felt real, but surely it had to be just a dream. If I told my mother about it, she would probably have me committed. I chuckled to myself; that was one crazy dream!

That's when I decided that I wouldn't even tell my friends. They would only think I was crazy, too, which a few of them already suspected. This would just confirm it. The matter was settled in my mind. I wouldn't speak of this place. It would be just that—a dream, one that didn't bear the worthiness of re-telling. I felt good for having settled this in my mind before my friends congregated in the clubhouse.

A few seconds later, Ryan came downstairs eating a bologna sandwich, and he decided to humor me with the bologna song.

"My bologna has a first name, it's O-S-C-A-R; my bologna has a second name, it's M-A-Y-E-R. Oooh, I love to eat it every day, and if you ask me why I'll SAAAAY—"

"Shut up," I interrupted.

I'd had enough, didn't want to hear any more. Besides, he seemed pretty normal, still the same troublemaker he'd always been.

"OK, but one day you won't say, 'shut up,' you'll be asking for my autograph," he boasted.

At first, I was shocked that he'd said that, but then I reminded myself it wasn't totally out of the ordinary. I had to let this dream go, I thought. So, to change the topic, I stated, "You might want to focus on how we gon' get ten good deeds done in basically a day."

"Let's just make up people," he suggested. *What?* I thought to myself, shocked again. He was still thinking like the same little boy; Learned Kansan hadn't changed him at all. Wait a minute, reality check — it was just a dream.

"The principal is going to be calling the people, remember? So, we just can't make them up."

From a distance, I saw Sharie walking down the block. Her mother had washed and oiled her hair, too, and she'd obviously had some sort of oil treatment as well. When she got closer, we signed greetings and she sat on the porch. Now there was someone else to witness how meticulously Ryan was eating his sandwich, savoring every bite. It made me want one, although I didn't really like bologna that much. It made my throat dry.

"So," signed Sharie, "did you get in trouble?"

"Oh yeah," I replied, "after today, one week with no television. Thanks, Ryan."

"You are welcome," Ryan replied sarcastically. "Me too, one week, but she'll cut it down. She can't do one hour with me, just the way it is."

"For sure," I agreed, for I knew that after a few days, my mother would be looking for other options as well.

We could see Stinky and Marion making their way to my porch. Marion always walked about two paces ahead of Stinky. This was his one way of communicating to the world that he wished he could leave him behind. He wouldn't tell his mother, it would just crush Stinky, and he wouldn't tell his dad for fear it would make him feel guilty for leaving them and might cause him to hurt someone in jail. So, he simply let the kid stick around—the little kid who hated to bathe.

We just sort of adopted him into our group, even though he was three years younger. I actually wasn't all that mad at the lil' dude today because he'd helped bring me back home. *Wait a minute—it was just a dream*, I scolded myself as Stinky and Marion joined our clique.

"So," I said to Marion, "did you guys get in trouble?"

"Nope. She just said we got to do what we got to do or we gon' be in detention all summer."

"Whoa," said Ryan. "For this reason, I love your mom. I not only want to marry her one day, but I want her to be my mom."

"Watch your mouth, Ryan, or I won't be your hype man," Stinky mouthed off.

"Then I would whoop your butt, 'cause I'd be your Daddy, son," Ryan shot back.

We all laughed. It was always funny to us how Ryan, this skinny red-headed kid, could think that one day a woman like Marion and Stinky's mother would actually give him some play. That was funny to me, and the rest of us, but what really stuck with me was that Stinky said *hype man*. Why did he say that? Did he know?

I quickly reminded myself that it was a dream again. One thing was certain, if Stinky had experienced anything close to what he'd experienced in my dream, he would have been bragging about it now. He would have certainly told Marion, and Marion would have told me because we tell each other everything.

We all headed to the back of the house where my father had built a wooden shed to keep all of his tools.

My dad still wanted a man cave and tool place, but the problem was people kept walking in and stealing his tools since he couldn't really lock it up. So, he stopped using it, and Ryan and I decided to fix the place up — painting it and all. Since no one really wanted us kids in the house, it became our outside hangout, our clubhouse — members only — and it's been that way ever since.

During the course of time, we sort of made this place home. Ryan keeps train sets and cars here. Marion gave us a black-and-white television set his dad used to watch in the kitchen. My mother, enjoying the fact that we could play someplace other than inside the house even when it rained, gave us an old love seat. We all found old chairs and stools to bring in, along with pictures we'd found from someone's garage and pop bottles we colored as decorations. We added an old lampstand we found somewhere and a chain of flashlights for when we wanted more light. It was our new home, our getaway spot, the place we were headed to so that we could somehow figure out how we were going to get ten people to sign our challenge sheet. We still wanted to have some kind of fun this summer. Well, at least we hoped.

27

THE PLAN

When we got to our place of comfort, we were silent for the first five minutes. We watched the flies buzzing around the small shed and listened to our own minds. I was hoping everyone was thinking of a plan—a way of getting back our fun, free summer—but I couldn't help wondering if maybe they were all thinking about Learned Kansan, like me. I really wanted to talk to them about it, but I didn't want anyone to think that I was going bonkers—that was Stinky's job. He's the one who makes the off-the-wall statements, leaving us all scratching our heads, thinking, *How did he come up with that?*

It was Marion who finally broke the ice. "We could go around to your dad's church and see if they need any help."

"Now that does sound like a good place to get a signature," I said. "Write that down."

Sharie was sort of our secretary. She was so good at reading lips, we rarely had to repeat ourselves. OK, we had one idea in the bag, only nine more to go. We looked at each other and at the time, which was moving faster than we would have liked. All we had was today, Saturday. Most people would be home or at some form of church on Sunday, so it had to be today. It was due Monday.

"Let's just walk," Sharie suggested, "and we can help people along the way. See, this way, good will just come to us!"

I stopped in my tracks, not because it wasn't a good idea, but because I knew it wasn't something that could have ever come to Sharie on her own. So, I questioned her.

"Where did you get that idea from?" I asked curiously.

"From my head," she signed with an attitude. She'd lied, and she knew that I knew it. That was not a Sharie idea. A Sharie idea is to steal a bike and take it back to the owner for the reward. A Sharie idea is to eat all the chicken and leave the bones, then blame it on the dog, forgetting that dogs love bones. To walk around and look for the good — that was not Sharie, not at all.

I was starting to think that somehow, we had all had the same dream or experience but we were all afraid to say anything about it. Was it because we didn't want the others to think we were crazy? Whatever the case, I was going to get to the bottom of it.

"Let's walk, shall we?" I said, but I wasn't going to just let this go.

We walked down the street and saw a lady struggling with untying her dog. Apparently, she had tied the knot too tight. We watched for a moment before we approached.

"Excuse me, madam, may I help you with that?" asked Ryan.

The lady looked over her glasses at us, eyeing us with suspicion. "And what do you little kids want for that?" She asked.

"Nothing. Well, really, we have to do ten good things for a project, so we just need your name and phone number." Ryan said.

"I'll see about that, but give it a try," she said in a skeptical tone.

Ryan and Marion went to work on getting the thing untied while Stinky played with the dog. It took at least ten minutes to free the dog, and Sharie and I were there all the way, cheering them on. They handed the dog back to the lady, and she gave them a twisted smile.

"If it wasn't for some shortiez stealing my dog and then giving it back to me for a reward, I wouldn't have had to tie that knot so tightly in the first place."

Nobody moved. Nobody gave the impression that at one time, that may have been our hustle. She took a pen out of her purse, signed our paper, and gave us her phone number. She still wasn't convinced that we just wanted to be helpful, but we didn't care. We had her signature.

"Did we ever do that to her?" asked Marion.

"No," we all admitted.

"Good. She's elderly; never hurt old people," Marion said.

"Never hurt people at all," I added.

Yes, we could be bad, but we were only out to have fun; we really didn't want to hurt anyone. We came to a fence that was being painted. The paint sprayer was already loaded up.

"We should paint this fence," said Sharie.

"Are you crazy? We can't do that," I responded.

"But we can and we should," stated Ryan.

I looked at the four pranksters, knowing that this wasn't going to end well. They had never used a spray gun before; this would be the first.

Attached to the spray gun was a machine that controlled the speed of the spray from slow, to faster, and finally to the fastest spray. It also allowed you to change the paint colors you were spraying, depending on what was loaded in the sprayer.

"Hurry up, we have to get the fence done before the man comes back out," said Stinky.

"I don't think this is a good idea," I warned.

"We're doing it," said Ryan, turning on the sprayer. Ryan put the speed on slow and Marion started actually painting the fence.

"Crank that thing up," said Stinky, "We got a lot more signatures to get!"

Ryan turned it up on high and the paint went everywhere! Marion yelled for help because the pressure was so high, so Ryan helped him hold the sprayer. It was as if the paint sprayer was lifting them off the ground. They painted the fence, the porch, and spots all over the house. It was funny until common sense kicked in, for this was the kind of stuff that earned us the reputation as "Dem Shortiez," and usually when this was said, it was not for good reasons. I turned off the paint spray just before a guy in overalls and a white painter's cap came out.

"Why, you kids!" He slammed his hands down on his porch and stormed toward us.

We were too frightened to move. Frozen in our tracks, we just stared at him, as if we had verbally given him permission to eat or kill us — we were just waiting for him to do something. When he got to the bottom of the stairs, he looked up at his house, and we watched with amazement as a huge grin came over his face. We slowly started breathing again.

"Did Martha send you? Oh! My honey told you exactly how to do it and I love it!"

The weird painter man was tearing up and we were too afraid to cry. The house looked like a crayon box had exploded on it. It wasn't ugly. It was just too disorganized to be purposeful. But this man seemed to think it was the most *be-yoo-ti-ful* thing he had ever seen.

"Um, thanks," I said.

We didn't know what else to say. We didn't really feel right watching an old man cry. Ryan and Marion, covered in paint, slowly backed away from the house. I motioned to Stinky to move back, but he was still looking at the house with all the wisdom in his eight-year-old head, trying to figure out what was beautiful about it. Sharie pulled on his arm, and he, too, started backing away from the house.

"Wait a minute," the man said, and we all thought that a sudden dose of reality had just hit him. "I mean, don't I owe you something for this beautiful creation? Anything?"

"Well, now that you mention it," said Stinky, "how 'bout twenty bucks?"

"No," I said, speaking over Stinky, "but can you sign this form for us, and include your phone number?"

"What? That's it?" the old man asked, looking at us strangely. "I've got money. I always keep me a little cash. I can pay you."

"Exactly —" Stinky was beginning to speak again, but I interrupted him.

"This was a school project, so to speak. We just need your signature and number." I gave the man the form and he signed and put his number on it. He also gave Stinky a twenty and then we all walked away.

"That guy was insane," said Ryan.

"I sort of liked it," said Marion.

We all stopped and looked at Marion, trying to make sure we'd heard him correctly, before walking to the food market.

At the food market, we got seven more signatures without much trouble. All we did was ask people if we could help them to their car, and they signed our form. We had nine signatures and only needed one more, but it was almost time for us to go home. We needed just one more person who needed help with bags or opening the car door—just one more person.

As we were sitting, collecting our thoughts, who drove into the food market but our own Principal Morten. He was driving his regular Ford pickup truck. He had on farmer's clothing as if he had just come from or was about to go to a farm.

"Let's ask Principal Morten if we can get away with one less signature," I suggested. "Maybe he'll accept just nine signatures instead of ten."

"He looks chipper," Marion responded.

So, with all the pity we could muster on our faces, we walked over, heads bowed, to Principal Morten's truck.

"What's the problem, kids? Why are you looking so down?" he asked.

"Well, our challenge form is due on Monday at nine o'clock, and we only have nine signatures. We worked all day, Ryan and Marion even painted a whole house, but we've run out of time and we didn't get ten. Could we turn it in with just nine signatures? Would that be enough? Please, we don't wanna go to public school or do detention."

He looked at our tired faces, and we hoped he could tell we were telling the truth. We had worked hard all day, accepting what was dished out to us. A couple of people even stiffed us: they took the favor we offered but didn't sign the form. We looked at Principal Morten, our eyes begging mercy.

"I'm sorry, kids, I said ten and I meant ten. You kids have had enough chances."

He walked into the store and picked up his items in a bag and then came back out, all while we were still standing there, not believing after all that we had gone through that we were still going to have to be in summer detention, probably with Mr. Howard, and public school in the fall.

I bet that was who would be working this summer, Mr. Howard. He'd make sure no one talked and everyone listened. That's what he always said, "No one talks and everyone listens." Then he would read something from his history book — something long and boring — and just to make sure we were listening, he'd give us a quiz on the spot. If we didn't answer the question correctly, we'd have to give him our seat until we answered the question correctly. He was a mean, horrible person, and I did not want to spend the summer with him. Besides, Mr. Howard's breath smelled like coffee and ashtrays on most days. On a good day, it smelled like cherry cola.

We watched as Principal Morten got back into his car and pulled out.

"Watch out, Principal Morten!" we yelled just before he hit a green pickup truck. He actually stopped barely an inch from hitting the truck.

That's what he gets, I thought to myself, *for not being generous. He could have let us walk with nine good deeds.* Principal Morten got out of his truck to make sure it was OK, then he looked over at us, totally surprised.

"Give me that form," he said.

We gave him the form and then he signed it and added his phone number as well.

"I don't want to receive any crank phone calls, you hear? Because I know who has my number, and I do have caller ID. I won't be there Monday. I arranged for Mr. Howard to watch over your clean-up project. You are not out of that. But you won't have to do detention, and no public school for you guys in the fall. I think you have learned your lesson. I am on my way to Learned Kansan so I can spend time on my uncle and aunt's farm for the summer."

When he said the words "Learned Kansan," we all jumped and moved three paces back from him and let out a gasp.

Wait a minute, was he Gill? I wondered. Nah, couldn't be. Gill was much better looking.

"Why are you guys looking at me like that? What, do you want to go to Learned Kansan with me?"

We all violently shook our heads no, terrified upon hearing the name of that place.

"Have a nice vacation," Ryan finally managed to say. We all nodded yes as if we were totally in agreement. Principal Morten just smiled at us and off he went.

"He said Learned Kansan," I whispered.

"I had a bad dream or something about that place," Marion confessed.

"Me too, I think," Sharie signed.

"Well, one thing's for sure," said Ryan, "no one wants to go there!"

"You got that right," agreed Stinky.

That was it. We were all too terrified to think that it could have actually been real. Could it have been some kind of weird common dream? As time went on, I discovered that I was the only one who remembered the dream almost completely. Marion remembered just running in a forest or something, Stinky remembered running from a bear who could talk, and Sharie remembered being told sweet nothings by some stranger in the woods. Ryan remembered dancing on the stage. But I remembered all of it.

I saw no need to share with them what I am now convinced was just a shared dream, probably based on some old tall tales Mr. Morten had told about the place he grew up. It was mysterious, but as my mother always said, there really is no such thing as mysteries. We were either just not the right people to unlock the mystery or maybe it was not the right time.

We walked back toward my porch, our meeting place for the next few months now that we had the summer off. At the end of the block, just before we got home, Stinky stopped in front of an old abandoned house and waved, looking curiously toward the upstairs window.

"Why you keep waving, ain't nobody in that old house," said Ryan.

"There *is* someone in that house, and she needs *rescuing!*"

"Well, then, go in there and get her and get yourself trapped," Ryan taunted.

"I *will* go in there, just you wait!" Stinky pouted.

We all stopped and looked at Stinky and watched as he simply kicked a rock in the direction of the house. As we turned to walk away, I caught a glance of a lady in the window. She had long black hair, straight like an American Indian, and she wore white. Maybe I should have said something at the moment, but I didn't. When I took a second look she was gone—but she was there, I'm sure of it. Anyway, we'd already had one adventure for the summer.

We made it back to my porch, and I don't know about anyone else, but I kept thinking that Stinky was right: something *was* in that old mysterious house at the end of the block. One day, we would surely have to go investigate, but not today. Today was our day off from solving mysteries. After all the adventure of the last few days, the only thing I really cared about was that I was home with my family and dem ride-or-die shortiez I call my friends.

ABOUT THE AUTHOR

Creola Thomas was born and raised in Chicago. *Adventures with the Shortiez: Portal to the Unknown World* is the first book in a three-book series. Creola's writing gives a front-row seat to the other side of the hood—the side where parents, even in poverty, raise their children with love and firmness. Her characters are deeply real, ripped from the pages of her childhood. Creola, in her own magical way, finds the joy and humor of growing up *hood*. She is a mother, a minister, and a teacher, as well as an advocate for adopted children and foster families. These books were written to not just entertain, but also to enthusiastically explain, explore, and inspire the wonderful imaginations of kids who grow up poor yet powerfully creative.